FROM THE AUTHOR OF 'LOVE CAN HAPPEN MULTIPLE TIMES'

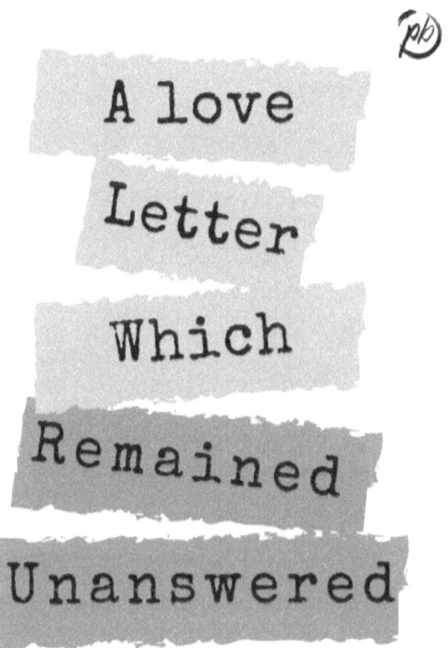

A love Letter Which Remained Unanswered

PRASAD R BATTU

PRASAD R BATTU

Thanks for buying my books

Contents

Preface

Love, I believe, is a very strong positive energy that cannot be destroyed or changed by any other negative energy.

There may be a failure of two people's understanding or a failure to meet each other, but there will be no failure of love, and love is pure, constant, and true to itself.

Love never fails, but people fail to understand the true meaning of love.

After a great response to my first novel, *"Love Can Happen Multiple Times,"* I began writing this novel. I am overwhelmed by all your love and support. I just didn't stop with the one, but decided to give you more and more entertainment every year. However, I can't match the love you showed me by doing anything in return, but I can give you good stories to read.

Before penning down any kind of story, I think in your perspective and start writing. I give more importance to your judgment than mine, because at the end of the day I am writing all these for you.

Reviews, feedback, comments and personal messages have been taken into account and improved my writing and explanation skills to entertain you.

Hope you enjoy this story as well as the first one.

Acknowledgments

I want to thank every reader of my first novel, '*Love can happen multiple times.*' Your support means quite a lot to me. Still, if you haven't read it, go and get your copy of it on Amazon.

I would like to thank my wonderful wife, *Swapna Battu*. From reading early drafts to offering me advice on improving my storytelling skills, she was as critical as I was in getting this book finished. Thank you so much, darling.

I would like to thank my friends who were my first readers here, and for their amazing feedback that led to the book being completed so quickly. Thank you for your time, *Dr Venkatesh Dasari* and *Sukanta Panigrahi.*

Shahla who is the book's super-woman, who with her editing skills was helpful and polite. She is the reason behind a well-tuned, error - free book and all the credit goes to her. You're the coolest, thank you *Shahla.*

Last but not the least, *'YOU,'* who bought it and encouraged me in writing another novel.

Prologue

'Wow..! You are stunning yaar, Shalu. You're looking awesome in the dark green saree! Are you getting married soon?' I had commented on Shalu's pic on Instagram with a 'Like' on it.

'Hey... George! Thank you so much for praising me dear, but, idiot! Without you getting married, how can I? Don't think too much' she replied to my comment. With a winking smiley,

I replied to Shalu, 'What's the link between my marriage and yours?'

While this conversation was going on, my phone buzzed. It was Ananya, my girlfriend. I picked up the call and said hello to her.

"What hello George?! What's happening with Shalu on Instagram? Why did you like her picture? And praising her too", she shouted.

"Hey! What's wrong with that? And why are you misunderstanding it? We have been friends since our childhood. Moreover she's looking good and lovely in the picture, so I just conveyed the same dear", I answered

"How can you compliment a girl in front of me, George? It's hurting", she said.

"What the hell is wrong with that, Ananya? I didn't say you weren't beautiful and I'm not going to compare you to her. You're a special person to me, dear. Why do you feel bad when I comment on a photo of a girl?" I asked.

"I don't know, you liked her photo and you praised her on social media. If any of my friends know anything about this… how can I deal with them now?" She started to cry.

"Hello! What the hell is wrong with you Ananya? Why are you crying for this little thing? Am I the first person to comment on a photo of a girl on social media? Moreover, I don't understand what it's like to feel bad and cry about it." I replied.

"I'm crying like a fool on one side, and you're saying it's a little thing? George, how bad you are! I think you've changed a lot and now you don't care about me as you did before. All because of that Shalu, I know you're cheating on me", she said.

"Ananya..! Wait! Have you lost your mind? I just liked her picture, I didn't do anything more than that. And there's no mistake in praising a girl. If I compare you with her, it's wrong. You're taking this particular issue to a different level. Please stop reacting to the little thing for God's sake." I said.

In the meantime, Shalu responded to the comment saying, 'Yeah. First, a handsome man like you should get married, and then the followers of you like us are going to get married in depression.'

What the fuck? Why is this girl creating more mess here? If Ananya sees this comment then I'm finished, I tried to console myself. God is so cruel. Why is he doing all this to me? Ananya checked Shalu's comment.

"George, tell me now! How can she comment like that without any affair? I think you both are in a relationship. You cheated on me. I've lost hope on you now. I am afraid what my situation would be after this", she started crying again.

"Arey..! Have gone mad Ananya? Shalu has been a friend of mine since childhood and she's a little closer, so she's having fun. How can you judge me by this single act of me on social media? You must be possessive of me, but this kind of inference is not acceptable at all", I said in frustration.

"Each time you do all these things and make me sob, you blame me again for all these things. I don't like you talking to any girl, even if she's a close friend of yours. I hate Shalu for this reason. Why she's making fun of you on the public platform all the time?" she said.

After listening to this, I got more furious and asked, "What's wrong with you? You stupid girl! Did I ever ask you when any of your friends comment on your photograph or when you comment or like someone's photo? No right? Huh? It's just because I have confidence in you and I know that you're not going to cheat on me. Shalu is the girl who has been helping us in our relationship since the very first day and how can you forget how she supported you in so many things in our early days?"

"Yes… I agree. She helped me with so many issues. But how am I supposed to ignore everything she does to you? See, she must be your childhood friend, yet now you both have grown up and if she continues to behave as she did in childhood, it won't look good at all, and everybody's going to spread rumours about both of you which I don't like." she replied.

"Ananya, I'm concerned about you, not about other people who talk bullshit outside. Because wherever there is a doubt, there will be no love. So, if you doubt me, please stop it right now. Once it hits your mind, it's going to keep growing and its better if we settle things now. It's going to be good for our relationship in the future" I said

"If you're concerned about me, I have a request for you, and if I ask you, you shouldn't get angry at me, okay? Sure, we just have to sort things out now, otherwise, it's going to run through my mind all the time", she said

"Request? What kind of request is it? And why would I get angry at you if it is a valid one?" I replied

"See, I'm asking you to stop talking to Shalu and unfollow her from all the social media accounts. I've even seen your WhatsApp chat with her where you had shared a few things about us that I didn't like. You must block her even in WhatsApp", she said

"Are you really nuts? Why did you check my mobile without my permission? But why is that? It's the height of stupidity, why do I need to stop talking to my friends who are with me way before you came into my life? When love demands to get away from my friends, I don't want that relationship. You're acting like a fool and messing it. I don't want you, please get out of my life", I yelled at her furiously.

"When you can't stop talking to a girl for me, I don't want you either. By trusting you, I've only been cheated at last" she started crying and hung up the phone.

Johnnie Walker

"Bro, wake up! Your destination is here", the Cab driver shouted.

Suddenly, I got up from my sleep. I thanked my cab driver and said bye to my cab mates and started walking towards my apartment. These days there are no calls from Ananya, no worries and I'm living a tension free life. I'm seeing my friends, spending time with them, and I started having a party on Saturday nights. Whenever I want to go out, I go without hesitation. So I realized why the singles were happy all the time without any tension.

I called one of my colleagues as it was a Friday night, I wanted to booze.

"Hello! Joseph Bro, can we call Johnnie Walker tonight to my apartment?" I asked.

"Dude… I was supposed to ask you at the office in the evening, but that dumb boss forced me to sit in an unnecessary meeting, so I got caught in that. Thank god you called me now", he said happily.

"So, where are you right now?" I asked.

"I'm in the office; where else can I be after having a fucking bastard as a boss? It might take more than 45 minutes here. He gave me some sheets to compare. Once I finish, I need to send him an email. I'm going to reach you in one and a half hour. In the meantime, please make the setup ready. Bro, Please prepare some Chicken Liver Fry, it tastes fucking awesome with a whiskey", he said.

I said alright and made a U-Turn to a wine shop to pick up Johnnie Walker. My mobile vibrated with a message. Joseph had made a transfer of Three Thousand rupees through Google Pay.

'Hey! Joseph, why did you transfer the money? Did I ask you?' I Whatsapped him.

'Chill... Bro! You just make all the arrangements and leave all the expenses on me. Now don't worry and concentrate on the masala in the Liver Fry', he replied with a winking smiley.

'Huh! You are a fool that never gives me an opportunity to spend anything on you. Complete the work quickly and throw it on the face of the boss and get to the room soon', I texted.

He replied okay to it.

I reached the Wines, where it's crowded as it's starting of a weekend night. So many people like us were already rushing to choose their preferred brand. Looking at them, I just didn't spare a second because if the stock of our favourite brand gets over, Joseph would kill me. I pushed the crowd, entered and picked it up. Yeah! Holding it in your hand gives you a kick and having it peg by peg gives you a double kick. I waited twenty minutes in the queue to pay the bill.

From there, I went to the chicken shop to pick the liver for the fry that Joseph specifically mentioned. Yeah. Finally, I took everything that was needed for a party. Right then, I only needed to get to the apartment soon and start cooking.

I was heading towards my home when I suddenly saw a wallet on the road near the chicken shop. I took it and checked nearby for the owner who lost it, but there was nobody around. I searched the wallet for any card or contact number, but no details were found. It had some Rs. 2571/-, ATM cards, withdrawal slips, and an old torn letter which had been taped so that it could not be further torn.

I couldn't find anyone there, so I put it in my pocket and started going home because if I sit there and look for the owner of it, I'm going to lose time and my party is going to be ruined. Joseph will kill me for sure.

I reached the apartment, freshened up and started cooking. The butcher hadn't cut the liver into pieces, so I had to cut them into pieces. I recalled Joseph's words about the extra *masala* in the fry. Then I added some extra ginger garlic paste, chilli powder, pepper powder, and garam masala. I mixed all the ingredients and kept them aside to set for some time.

I had kept the soda in the fridge to keep it cool until Joseph hits. I chopped the onions and the chilies for the Fry. Cooking for yourself is a very satisfying job, that too for a snack at the time of drinking. After a long busy day, I got double the energy to prepare it because it's the weekend and Johnnie Walker is waiting. After thirty minutes of marinating, I tested the mixture. It was well balanced and the aroma spread throughout the kitchen after opening the lid of the pot.

I couldn't resist the thought of eating it, so I started cooking it right away. Twenty-five minutes later, I cooked it and finished a plate of liver fry before Joseph came in.

It was all set for a party and just to build a party mood, I dimmed the lights and called Joseph to ask where he was?

"Hello Bro..! Where are you now? Mr. Johnnie Walker along with liver fry is waiting for you. It's driving me towards it now. I can't control myself, my brother", I said.

"George, I just got out of the office and am waiting for a taxi, it's on the way. By the way, did you get cigarettes bro?" He asked.

"No, Bro..! I skipped it in order to pick.... don't mind. Please get one packet of cigarettes when you come" I said.

"Hey! Chill bro! Don't worry, I'm going to get some", he said.

"Great man! Please come soon, my tongue just can't resist getting some booze right now" I said.

"You son of a bitch! It's only two days from the last time we had. Wait for me, don't be in a hurry," he exclaimed.

"Hehe!" I grinned sarcastically and said alright and hung up the phone. Now I had no choice but to wait for Joseph. So I turned on the TV. India Vs New Zealand T20 match replay was being telecasted on Star Sports. So I started watching it. Around 11:00 PM Joseph reached the room.

"Hello, my dear George, let's just rock the party! Is everything ready?" he just jumped over and asked.

"Huh...I almost dried up waiting for you, dude. Why this much time, huh? See poor Johnnie Walker, how he is looking at me," I said with a sigh.

"All right... I apologize to Mr. Johnnie Walker. Just give me five more minutes, I'm going to get fresh and then we'll start" Joseph said.

We both started drinking peg by peg. After a few rounds, Joseph began to scold our boss for showing him hell and not allowing him to get out of the office on time and for dumping more work.

"Calm down macha, not just the developers' team boss is like that but our project manager is also the same. But he's not going to disturb me, because in the whole project, I know A to Z about it. If he disturbs me, he knows clearly that I'm going to put down my papers, so he's not going to play with me", I said.

"You're such a smart macha. If you put down your papers, you're going to get a job the next day, but my case is different, I can't fight with my boss. That's why I'm working late. Whatever he says, I'm listening" Joseph said.

"Huh... It's not about smartness, but how you handle the things", I said.

"Let's leave this topic man, I'm going to get angrier if we keep talking about it", Joseph answered with a low voice.

"Okay man", I said. We had completed half of the Johnnie Walker by that time.

"Hey! George, how is Ananya doing? No calls these days and you are boozing very relaxed without any disturbance?" Joseph asked.

"Don't just spoil my mood by talking about her now. We broke up for some stupid reason", I explained it all to him

"Oh..! These girls never change dude, they're going to doubt us for each and everything. Yet your pair looked fantastic", he replied

"Hey, pour me a peg dude. There's no fry left in the bowl, I'm going to get the rest of it from the kitchen," I said. He came with me too, stood in the balcony and lit the cigarette.

"George, what's your opinion on Mahira?" he asked all of a sudden.

"Dude, she's just a stunning beauty yaar. Damn sexy, man and she's the fantasy of our entire office" I said.

"Yeah… true. But, you know something? While the whole office has been dreaming about her, she fell for you. If you ask, she will die for you", he said.

"Don't make me a fool, man. Where is her beauty and where I am! And how come a beauty fall for an idiot guy like me", I said.

"The whole office is jealous of you. They all know about that. Don't you know that?" he asked shockingly while finishing off a cigarette. We went back to the hall with a bowl full of liver fry.

"Don't know bro, if this is serious then I am the fool who missed this chance to romance her for so many days", I responded with a cynical smile.

"Yeah, man. Some of our colleagues are already circulating the story that you've had sex with her", he said.

"I'm not that lucky man, I didn't even realize that she likes me. I just got to know that now. But let me speak to her tomorrow and if she's all right, I'll invite her to my house. We will enjoy two days here to the core" I said with a smile.

"George, you're too quick to make a decision. If she complains about you that you asked her to have sex with you, then what would be your position in the office?" he asked alarmed.

"Don't worry mate! I'm going to take care of that. I know how to talk to her about it. You've already given me a clue that she likes me, so my path is clear," I said.

"Yet, I'm still worried," he said.

"Don't worry man, just leave that thing to me and focus on Johnnie Walker right now," I said.

It was around 02:00 AM, when we had finished. Joseph said he was going home. So, I said, "Dude…It's already late, just sleep here." He agreed.

Since we had finished the full bottle of whiskey, we fell asleep in no time.

Blind Date

It's very difficult to clean a room after a party. I woke up around 10:00 AM with a hangover. Joseph woke up after 20 minutes. He freshened up and went to his house. I started cleaning the room after he left. It took about two hours to clean everything. I had a bath and cooked a meal for myself for lunch.

I remembered our conversation about Mahira. Yes. She was really sexy. As every one of us describe a beautiful girl with 36-24-36 dimensions, she also had the same perfect figure. Who wouldn't fall for her incredible physique. I called her to talk to clarify myself about what Joseph said last night. To my surprise, she answered my call on the very first ring.

"Hello... Hey handsome! How come you called me today?" she asked in a husky voice.

"Hi Mahira! How are you doing? I just wanted to talk to you, so I called you," I said.

"Arey Baba, yesterday we had met and now you're asking for my well-being. How formal you are, George.

What do you want to talk about by the way? Huh?" she whispered.

When she asked that, I was not able to say a word. If I asked her directly, I didn't know how she would react and that kind of thing is very new for me to deal with? I had told Joseph confidently in the night but now I was empty for a moment.

"Hey Dude! What happened? Why are you so silent?" she asked. Then I recovered and replied to her, "Mahira have you got a boyfriend?" I asked.

"Hey... Dude..! What happened now? Why are you questioning me about my boyfriend?" she asked.

"Nothing happened, I just wanted to see him. Since you're so stunning, how amazing he would be?" I replied.

"You brazen man! Don't you think you're flirting directly with me?" she said.

"No yaar, I'm serious about that. You look very stunning and so your boyfriend has to be a handsome hunk," I said.

"It's not necessary George. A simple man with a loving heart always suits a beautiful girl. You guys think beautiful girls won't fall for a simple guy but they really like simple guys," she said.

"Oh! Is it? So a simple guy like me can try for a girl like you, right?" I questioned.

"Yes, of course. But what happened to you all of a sudden?" she asked curiously.

"Nothing. All I need is a favour from you. I'm going to ask you something if you're not going to feel bad about it," I said.

She asked, "What is it? Now I got the tension."

"Don't worry. I just need some details, that's it. If you could support me with that, it would be fantastic," I said.

"Okay. I'm going to help you for sure. But what kind of information is that, sir?" she asked mockingly.

"Mahira, I know a girl, she's a stunning beauty like you and I know she likes me. So I wanted to call her for a date. How can I approach her?" I asked.

"Hey Dude, are you sure about that? But you have a girlfriend already? Why this relationship again? If your girlfriend gets to know about it, then what?" she asked.

"Don't think about that, I broke up with Ananya. It's just a date with this girl. And these days, you know right, it's all normal. Just one thing- both of them have to be in an agreement," I said.

"You never told me that you broke up with Ananya. I would have proposed you," she said laughing.

"Why are you joking with me?" I said even though I understood her intentions.

"I'm not kidding George, I've had a crush on you but I never told you that because you were already in love with Ananya" she replied.

"Oh my god! Are you serious? You are the fantasy of the whole company and you like me?" I asked as if I didn't know anything about it.

"I know a lot of people are trying to impress me, but you've never acted like that" she said.

"Okay, now if I ask you for a date, will you agree?" I asked.

"George, are you joking with me? That beautiful girl you wanted to call for a date is me, isn't it?" she asked.

"Yes, but only date, no other relationship. If you agree to that then we can go ahead," I said.

"You Idiot, do you get that? You are asking me to have sex with you openly," she said.

I got scared with her response and thought that she must have been angry and that she's probably going to complain to HR about me. I was confused. What should I say, 'yes' or 'no'? Both were complicated responses. If I said YES and she didn't like it, then my job is gone. If I said NO and if she likes to do it, then my chance is gone. What to do then? No matter what happens, I decided in my mind that I'll say YES only and face the circumstances later.

"If you're all right about it, we should commit," I said.

"You're a stupid ass! Is it the way to ask a girl for it? And you've taken a lot of time to ask me. You know I'm engaged now and after two months, it's my marriage," she said.

Oops, man. It was a very bad time to ask, really.

"I'm so sorry, Mahira. I didn't really know you were engaged. Otherwise, I wouldn't have asked you to do that," I said.

"Hey. In fact, I'm very happy. At last you've dared to ask me. I wanted to go on a long drive with you but you never offered me a place to discuss it with you. If you had given me time, we must have had many good moments by now," she said.

I didn't understand it. If she didn't want it, she should have cut off the conversation. But she kept going. She must be trying to give me a hint to ask her again. So, in my head, there was a clear idea to ask her again.

"Mahira, you're engaged yeah! And it's your marriage after two months. I am the one whom you loved. So why don't we commit it once before you get married? And how can your future husband know about it? There's no algorithm or measure for them to know whether you had sex or not before you got married," I said.

"I don't think you must have been slapped by anyone until now, that's why you're talking to me like that. But what you said is true too. I'd love to do it. Yet, when and where?" she asked

Again it was an 'Oh My God' situation for me. I didn't expect her to accept that. I wanted to share this with Joseph because he was the only reason for me to talk to her, and unexpectedly, even though she was engaged, she accepted it. Yet I took control of myself and kept quiet.

"Mahira, Are you serious about accepting it? I can't believe it. If you're sure of that then I'm going to come and pick you up from your PG. You can stay right here in my house. We will enjoy it for two days," I said.

"I'm serious about it, Mr. Romeo. Meet me by 03:00 PM. I'll be ready by then. Today, we can go and rock it," she said.

I disconnected the call, cleaned the house very quickly, prepared the bedroom and sprinkled the lilly fragrant room fresher to make the atmosphere fresh and romantic. I got ready and applied ZARA perfume and went out to pick her up. Before reaching, I went to a nearby medical shop to grab some condoms. I picked some different ones because I didn't have much experience. So, to test which one is comfortable, I picked different types and flavours. The medical shop guy gave me a weird look.

I reached her PG and asked her to come outside. It was drizzling outside. Even the climate was favouring the situation and making the atmosphere more romantic. But because of the stress, my pulse had doubled. It was a sort of tension I had never felt before. I didn't know why it was happening, but I felt like I was going to die there out of fear.

I was shivering actually, which only I could sense and nobody else. She came out with a backpack wearing a dungaree jeans top. She looked damn sexy and hot in the unique outfit.

"Hey… Mr. Romeo, are you ready for the war?" she asked me in a husky voice.

Without looking into her eyes, I said hello. Out of stress or shyness, I didn't know why but I couldn't look at her.

From there we started, she sat on the bike hugging me. My body began to vibrate with her touch. She asked me about the food plan, whispering from her mouth and biting my ear. It was a nice feeling but I asked her to contain herself until we got to the house.

"George… It's been a long time that I have been waiting to eat you, how more can I still wait? I've been waiting for this day for so long, and now you're asking me to wait. I don't care about the people around us, you just drive to your house soon," she said.

"Alright…I'm going to drive you there as soon as possible, but please stop biting my ear, it's paining," I said.

"Man…It's just an ear, and now you've got more painful things to face. Don't you know that?" she asked.

"Painful, huh? Okay, what is it? I don't know," I said, concerned.

"Let's get home first, then I'll tell you what it is," she responded.

I said okay. We grabbed some pizza and coke on the way. Because I didn't want to waste any time coming out for food again.

We walked into the room and she just grabbed me from the back and started pulling off my T-Shirt.

'Hey… Mahira, just relax, we've got a lot of time. You just settle down first," I said.

"Chal… Drop the T-shirt idiot, why wait? Let's play our first game right now. After that I'm going to settle," she slapped me and said.

"Ouch… It's a painful yaar, why did you slap me? I'm removing it," I said, rubbing my cheek.

"Oh my baby, is that hurting you so badly? Is it so painful?" she started to rub my cheek gently with her hands and kissed it. It wasn't my first kiss, I and Ananya had kissed many times. But I felt this was different. It was like I was using someone else's stuff without paying for it.

"George… You sprayed Lilly flavoured room spray to offer more essence of romance right?" she asked.

"Yeah," I said and started removing the buttons on her dress straps.

"This is all right, but did you get some safety?" she asked.

"Yes… of course. But I don't know what to choose, I've got a lot of them," I showed her all the packets of condoms.

"Man, do you want to open a shop or what with all these?" she started laughing.

"No problem. We can use these for future meetings," I said.

"Okay, that means what? Do you think I will be here for you all the time? No way, whatever you want to play, just for today and tomorrow. I'm not coming later," she said.

"Okay we can think about the future later, let's start the game now," I said.

Her skin tone had a beautiful blend of colours. And her physique was the real meaning of elegance. Anything I wanted to do was to leap into her beauty and devour it completely. I sat on the bed, pulling her waist up and made her sit on my lap with her legs spread towards me.

Each inch of our body was touching each other and we had nothing on our bodies. I took the band out of her hair and held it, pulled her to me and kissed her lips. While kissing, I could see that her eyelids were closing in slow motion. That's the essence of romance, you can't feel it if you see it.

It lasted for five minutes and I sucked all of her saliva into my mouth. It tasted good with a flavour of mint. Before coming here, she must have had mint-flavoured chewing gum. Okay, I could sense that.

"George… I can't wait any longer now, please let's do it," she started moaning and asking for it. I just opened a random pack of condom and took one from it and ripped the pack away. She took it quickly and made me wear it. I was wearing it for the first time and it had some kind of gel on it which was very slippery. I pushed her to the bed and jumped on her.

We started experiencing the essence of sex. She started moaning a little louder and shouted to move it slower.

"George… You've got more time, don't use all your strength just now, you've got to keep a little more energy that's going to last until tomorrow night," she said moaning.

"Yeah," even though my AC was running, I was sweating rigorously and breathing heavily, responding to her, "I've got a lot more strength, it's going to last a long time."

We have had the first glimpse of it. Immediately, I could see bloodstain on the bed sheet. After seeing it, I panicked.

"Hey… Mahira. What's the blood in here? What happened? Have I hurt you?" I asked her tensed.

"Nothing to worry about, George. This is the first time we are doing it, right? There's going to be a little blood. Now it is a painful bloody friendship between us," she said and kissed my lips.

After that, we washed ourselves, ate pizza and went to bed. Then we had sex countless times until the next night. Both of us were happy about it.

A Letter

I got ready to go to the office after a hectic romantic weekend. The time I spent with Mahira was in my mind. It would have been good if a weekend lasted for a week, we would have enjoyed more time. The crappy idea lurked in my head.

While I was packing my stuffs in my bag, I noticed the wallet that I had found on the road which I had totally forgotten about. I thought of reading the letter which was in the wallet but I was completely struck by Mahira's romance.

Now, I had to go to work, so, I put the wallet back in the bag and rushed. It was 08:45 AM and at any moment my cab would arrive. Before it came, I had to finish my sandwich as well as wear my shoes.

I had breakfast, then went down and waited for the cab. I wanted to call Mahira, but we had agreed each other not to talk again about what happened in the last two days. If at all both of us felt like meet again, we had to keep it going secretly. That was the agreement we had, so I didn't call her.

I boarded the cab, put on the earphones and started listening to Alan Walker's songs. After a while, I remembered the letter and opened the bag and took it out. It was almost torn. I opened it carefully and I held it with the support of my diary.

The letter was written on 21 February 1982. It was written by Ms. Bhoomi Sharma addressed to Mr. Sameer Mohammad. Interestingly, this purse belonged to Mr. Sameer Mohammad. Yet why was he still keeping it in his wallet? Without keeping it safe at home.

More surprising was that the letter was written by a Hindu girl to a Muslim boy. So what happened next? Why was he still carrying it? There were so many questions in my mind. So, I started reading it to get the answers.

Date: 21st February 1982

To,

Sameer Mohammad,

Street Number 5, Dwaraka Nagar.

Vishakhapatnam.

Dear Sameer,

It's been three months since we were separated from each other. Every day I spend every second in remembrance of you. My father forced me to get married. He trusted that fool more than me. I was trying to explain to him, but he was not ready to listen to me at all.

I had made it clear that I was going to die, but never marry anyone other than you. He still didn't understand and acted like a fool. We know we've never seen our religions, our caste, or our wealth. We are very true to our feelings and we have cherished them, and we have not gone beyond our limits. Yet we didn't have the opportunity to explain it.

I don't understand, however, that whenever the celebration of Ram Navami happens, you have come and taken part in the Pooja and at the time of Ramadan Roza, we had served you with Iftar without differentiating our religions. But when it comes to a true feeling, why are they dragging caste and religion into it?

If we honour our traditions and help each other, why can't a Hindu girl marry a Muslim guy? Every day, I argue with my dad about this. But he doesn't have an answer. But he says that since the elders followed it, we 're to do the same. How dumb is he?

After all this fight between our two families, you've moved to another location. After a lot of query, I got your address from your mate, Girish, with the help of Ranga. Now I'm writing this letter with a lot of pain and sadness. I don't know what's going to happen to my life without you. But I'm hoping for a nice and happy end to our relationship.

Please reply to me after reading this letter and send me information about coming to me through Girish. I will be ready and waiting for you, I'm not going to live here, whatever it is. I'm just going to be with you.

I will be waiting for you. I Love You.

Yours,

Bhoomi Sharma,

Plot No. 2A, H No. 4F/2,

Ram Nagar, Kothavalasa,

Vishakhapatnam.

After reading the letter, I understood one thing that, Sameer had got this letter but what happened after that? Did he go to her? What happened then? Did they get married, or not? I really wanted to know the answer to so many questions and the rest of the story. But how? The letter was written almost 38 years ago. Where could I find these people now?

I found the letter close to my house which suggests that Sameer must live near my place. But where to look and whom to ask? Finding a single person in this busy city is very difficult but it is also not possible to find a person without much hints. I could go to the address mentioned in the letter and connect the dots to find them.

I figured that God had to have some plans for me which was why I had found this letter. And I was very curious to know about the love story of those two people. I planned to go to Vishakhapatnam in the weekend. It was going to be a real adventure.

Doing this kind of detective work with a small hint like a letter was giving me goosebumps. I felt like Sherlock Holmes and I started thinking about the weekend. I told the same thing to Joseph who was also very excited and he joined me to go to Vizag. We booked our tickets to Vizag.

Hello Vizag!

We both boarded the Garib Rath Express from Secunderabad at 8:00 PM. There were a lot of questions in my mind. Is it a right idea to travel to Vizag? I couldn't understand. But since I had already decided to visit, I decided to go and face our fate. If I can meet Bhoomi there, then I could understand the whole story of what happened after the letter.

"Dude, are you sure that we're going to meet that lady?" Joseph asked.

"I don't know, but if we meet her it's going to be a great journey for us," I said.

"Yeah. If we weren't able to find her, it would be a great disaster," he said.

"Whatever be the result, we will be satisfied that at least we tried," I said.

"Damn, I've never done this thing before, it's crazy," he said.

At around 10:30 PM, the train reached Warangal Railway Station. I got down to grab a cool drink.

"Hey Joseph! Do you want bread omelet? It will be very good at this station," I asked.

"Yes, bro, of course. Why not?" He answered.

I bought two bread omelets and a Thumbs Up, and got into the train. We sat in the lower berth and was having it. The uncle sitting opposite to us was gazing at us. At first, I couldn't understand why he was looking, but then, it flickered my mind that the lower berth was confirmed to him. He was waiting for us to finish it and move to our berths so that he could take a nap.

We completed it very quickly because if we delayed further, he was going to throw us out of the train. We quickly climbed to our confirmed upper berths. Then they all fell asleep in a span of seconds and turned off the lights. The train was running at its maximum speed. I switched on the songs on my mobile phone and put on my earphones and was asleep in a few minutes.

It was around 7:00 AM when everybody was rushing and I got up disturbed in the hustle. By the time, Joseph had woke up and was watching videos on his mobile phone. The train crossed the Duvvada station, and we were about to reach Visakhapatnam in forty minutes. I got down from the berth and went and stood by the door.

Early in the morning, the cool fresh breeze gave a very comfortable welcome. With that, I felt very hopeful. Somewhere in my subconscious mind, it said that I was going to meet Bhoomi.

Everybody rushed with their luggage to get close to the door. I can't understand the mentality of the people. They just drive everyone at the time of boarding to get into the train. They're going to do the same to get down, too. But why is that? If they had reserved seats, it'll only be reserved for them, no other person can sit in them even if they get late by two minutes. The train will stop here only which is the last station. They're running to get down as if it is a race.

Eventually, the train reached Visakhapatnam. We got off the train and walked out of the station. We took an OYO room first, freshened up and went to *Sri Ram Parlour* in Dwaraka Nagar to have breakfast.

At the time of starting from Hyderabad, one of our office mates from Vizag had told us about a few places from where we should not miss a meal. *Sri Ram Parlour* was one of those locations.

We had ordered Ghee Karam Idly and as my friend said, it melted in the mouth and tasted amazing. We finished each of the three plates.

After listening to the name, 'Dwaraka Nagar', I recalled Sameer. After the incident, he moved from Kothavalasa to this place. But now he's staying somewhere in Hyderabad. If we search for him here in Dwaraka Nagar, we won't be able to find him. So we decided to go first to Bhoomi's place.

We finished breakfast and took the Auto and began to get to Kothavalasa. We tried to check the address with the auto driver. He said he didn't know the exact address, but he took us to Ramnagar where Bhoomi stays in Kothavalasa.

We got down and thanked him and stood there and watched the area from where we had to start our search. Usually, addresses will be known to paper boys or milk boys. So, we walked into a nearby pan shop to get the number of the paperboy.

He asked us so many things like, who are we, where we were coming from, why we needed all these details, etc. Joseph was terrified. But I just cooked a story that Bhoomi was my grandmother and we came from the

United States to see her. We were not able to trace her because we only had an address. Other than that we had no other information. So, the innocent guy believed the whole story and gave the contact number of the paper-supply guy who distributes to the Ram Nagar Area.

I called that guy, he picked up our call and after listening to us, he asked us to get nearer to Hanuman Temple. He checked the address and said that no one lived there in that name and that the address was also not correct. He said, "We have very rare independent houses in this location. All the apartments are built. So we need to check with the plot number."

At last, we reached Plot No. 2A. It was a large apartment now and we were filled with the expectation that we were going to meet Bhoomi in any one of the flats.

We thanked the paper guy and gave him five hundred rupees for his support. He refused to take it, but we gave it. We walked towards the gate and called the apartment guards and asked about Bhoomi. He said that he didn't know anyone there in that name. I explained to him that she must be about sixty years old now and that her full name is Bhoomi Sharma, who loved a Muslim man named Sameer in 1982.

He said, he didn't know anything about the story, but could ask his grandfather about it, who had lived in that area at that time. He offered us a chair and a cup of tea and went outside to get his grandfather.

We explained the story to the elder man and surprisingly, he recognized them.

"Well, what's your name son?" he asked me.

"George,' I replied.

"George, huh?" He asked confused.

"Yes, George... Uncle, is there any problem with that name?" I asked him.

"There's no problem, my son. Bhoomi is a Hindu girl, and how come her grandson's name is George? I got confused," he said.

"Hey, wait a minute. I'm not her grandchild. You've got me wrong. In fact, a week ago, I found a letter written by Bhoomi to Sameer. So, to know their story, I came here," I said.

"All right, but she's not here right now. After the incident, they left the city. I don't know where they are and what they're doing, yet I know one of her classmates. I'm going to take you there, check with her. If we can get the details that will be good," he said.

We agreed to go there and meet her. Since the time was around 02:00 PM, they offered us lunch. We refused it politely at first, but they asked us to accept it. We finished lunch and started to Bhoomi's friend's place.

Grandpa told us to stay downstairs and he went up to meet her. He returned within five minutes. I was eagerly waiting for some details about Bhoomi from her friend. But she wasn't in the house and would only get back the next day. So he gave us her details and asked us to come and check with her tomorrow. We thanked him for the lunch and the support he gave us and went back to the room.

We were exhausted from the journey and looking for her the full day. So we had a nap in the evening when we reached the room. We woke up around 8:00 PM., got ready quickly and went to the Alpha Biryani Center in Jagadamba Center. I was a very crowded area and we had to wait forty-five minutes for our turn. We had a tummy full of Chicken Biryani and went back to the room and slept waiting for the next morning.

Around 11:00 AM, we reached the address of Bhoomi's mate. We rang the bell and an elderly lady came out and opened the door.

"What are you selling man? We don't need anything, move on," she scolded us.

"Ma'am, we don't sell anything. Actually, we've come to meet you to know more about Bhoomi," I said.

She was in a shock for a while. She invited us into the house after coming out of it.

"Who are you, huh? And how do you know Bhoomi? Why are you asking for her details?" she asked.

I explained the whole thing that happened last week.

"Are you sure about that? Does that letter have you here? And when you know Sameer, why don't you ask him specifically what happened after that," she said.

"We don't know Sameer either, I found this letter on the street and I started looking for both of them, and I got to Vizag," I said.

"Okay, now I've understood everything. So after reading the letter, you've found it fascinating and you've come here to enquire whether or not they've gotten married. Fine. Good. Yet Bhoomi isn't in Vizag right now, she's in Hyderabad," she said.

I was surprised. But how? What the heck is she doing in Hyderabad? I asked, "Where in Hyderabad is she living? They got married, huh? What happened actually?"

"We don't know whether she married Sameer or not. They moved to some other place in Vizag after the fight, and later she didn't meet anyone. We tried a few times to find her and meet her, but none of our friends could find her. Suddenly, one year ago, she came to Vizag and met us. She told us that she was running the old age home in the Begumpet area in Hyderabad and that she was staying there as well. We asked her about her marriage and her children, but she didn't talk about it. This is the only thing we know about her, other than that we don't know anything," she said.

We noted the address from her and started back to Hyderabad.

Bhoomi's Place

I had to wait another week to get to the old age home where Bhoomi was living. I was very curious to meet her, to know her story? Why was she living in an old age home? What happened to her family? etc.,

Joseph came to my room on Friday night, as he was also interested to meet her. At night, we held a small party and the whole topic was Bhoomi and Sameer. The key question was about what had happened after the letter.

We were really shocked that in this digital age, if any small mistake or fight happened between lovers, we blocked them and erased all their memories. But look at the letter that Bhoomi wrote to Sameer. He kept it carefully for 38 years. It's called true love.

We finished the party but I could not sleep. The only thing that ran in my mind was Bhoomi and Sameer. I looked at the clock and it was running really slow. Joseph was already asleep. I got up from the bed and started to walk and think about the next morning when we meet Bhoomi. What should I ask her? I was thrilled to meet her.

Even after seeing the letter for the first time, Sameer would not have felt this way.

Thinking all these things, time was still moving very slowly. I had to get up early to go to Begumpet, so I convinced myself and went to bed.

Time was 11:00 AM.

Suddenly, I got up as if someone screamed loudly in my ears saying, "You fool, you will get late to meet Bhoomi." I realized that this man, Joseph, didn't get up either and all the plan was going to get screwed today. I kicked his ass and said, "Get up and get ready".

We got ready and started to go to Begumpet. By the time we reached the Old Age Home, it was around 1:30 PM. The gatekeeper stopped us while entering in.

"Sir, where are you going?" he asked us.

"Hey, we're here to meet Ms. Bhoomi Sharma," I replied.

"Oh, Bhoomi ma'am. But, sir, the hours of access are over now. You need to come tomorrow again. We only allow visitors to reach them in the morning from 10:00 AM. to 12:00 PM.," he answered.

We were shocked to wait for another day. We both stared at each other's faces.

"Bro… bro… see we've come to meet Ms. Bhoomi all the way from Vizag, now if you ask us to come back tomorrow, it's going to be hard for us as we're having a train back tonight," I cooked a story again to get an entry.

"Sir, you don't understand my problem. Bhoomi madam is very strict when it comes to timings and you're asking me to speak to her to get you to meet her. It's very challenging sir," he responded irritated.

First, after knowing about her strict punctuality, I got scared. If she's so particular about timing, would she be willing to tell her story? Are we wasting our time? It was all running in my head.

"Bro… don't worry, I will make sure that you don't get scolded. You just give her this letter. Definitely she'll give us the access. Please do us this one favor," I asked.

"Hmm… Sir, I understand that you have decided to have me thrown out of this position. I don't know whose face I saw while I was getting up this morning. Give me that letter," he grabbed the letter, and went in.

We were waiting eagerly for him to come out. He came out running within minutes. First of all, we were concerned because he was racing fast when he returned and also many questions were floating in my mind. We didn't know the background but we had assured him quite confidently that nothing was going to happen to his job.

He was panting, "Sir, sir! What was on the letter?" He was panting breathlessly. After his pause, our heart began to race faster. "What happened bro? What did she say?" I asked him.

"Sigh... after reading the letter she just started crying and immediately asked me to take you to her," he answered.

After knowing that she called us to talk, I felt very pleased. We went inside without wasting a minute.

It was a very long room filled with books and an iPod in the corner playing Sir. Mohammad Rafi's songs at a very low volume. I saw a picture of a young man wearing a vintage costume with long hair, a beard and big glasses on the wall. There was an arm chair and a bed and nothing more in the room.

As we walked into the room, she immediately began to touch us gently with wet eyes. First of all, we didn't understand why she was crying and doing that. But as an elderly woman staying at old age home, she would be missing her family, so we kept it going and waited for her to talk.

She told us to sit down on the bed and asked the watchman to get some snacks and juice for us, as it was afternoon and we had come in from the hot sun.

We settled down on the bed and she sat on the chair. I was waiting for her to start talking about the letter. I didn't know how she was going to take it if I asked her about the letter. So I waited for her to start.

"Where did you get this letter from? I wrote this letter to my Sameer in 1982. This is the best memory of us. I recalled all our memories back again after I saw it. But how do you know I live here? And who are you both?" she started asking us questions. I explained everything that had happened to us in the past 20 days after I found the letter.

"Oh! So sweet of you! After you've seen this letter, you traveled to meet me to know the rest of the story. Great.!" she said with a gentle smile on her face. "Still, um...! What are you going to get after you know the rest of the story? Why would you like to hear about it?" she asked.

"As you are the age of our grandmother, may we call you Granny? Because we don't want to call you by name," I said.

"Yeah, yeah! Of course, I'm going to be happy to be called Granny," she said.

"Granny, I've got a girlfriend. We just broke up for a stupid reason. We, this generation, are breaking our love for no reasons but after reading that letter, I understood how deep your love would still be to hold on to that letter. This is why we care about your beautiful love story. Say, granny, what actually happened? Where did it begin and what happened after the letter?" I asked.

Akashvani - Vishakapatnam

Akashvani-Visakhapatnam Station, playing the song *' Ye Teega Puvvuno'* from the movie *' Maro Charithra'* sung by Kamal Hasan and P Susheela.

It was raining heavily outside with thunderstorms. My father, Thrinath Sharma was on a call speaking in a high tone and scolding them. My father was a local leader in the town. He did all the settlements. The call was also about some land settlement, they were supposed to go somewhere to settle things but because of the storm, one of his closest followers didn't turn up.

"Hey Ranga! Where's Moin Bhai? Didn't he turn up until now? These sons of a bitch are not listening to us for this land registration. We have to give our treatment, only then they will understand. Find out where Moin is right now!" my father screamed.

"Okay, boss," Ranga said and ran to the gate.

While all this was going on, I was sitting in the hall, enjoying the rain and the song on the radio. Ranga entered the house again shouting that Moin Bhai was coming. Then I saw Sameer coming home to drop his father on a Bajaj Chetak. I had known Sameer since childhood, but I never felt it as differently as that day. Sameer was absolutely drenched in the rain. He had long hair and a small beard, and very beautiful eyes with a faint innocence.

He parked the vehicle and came and stood out on the verandah where my father and his father were talking about the case. One of our maids gave him a towel to dry himself.

"Son, you be here till the rain stops. We're heading out now, I might get back late. So, as soon as the rain stops, you go back home," Moin said to Sameer. Sameer nodded at Moin.

Then my father and his father along with a few of their followers went out. Sameer sat on the verandah table. I called my maid and asked her to give him some hot tea. When the maid took him the cup of tea, she showed me and told him that I had asked her to give him the tea. He gave me a *salaam* with a gentle smile on his face as a grateful gesture. That was our first direct eye contact then.

He began reading a newspaper while having tea. I came out of the hall and sat on my father's chair. He stood up as gesture of reverence for me.

"Hi! Why are you standing? Be free. No one's going to scold you, don't worry. Treat me as your friend Sameer," I said.

"How do you know my name?" He asked me with a surprised look.

"When your father was speaking to you, I was listening and I'm not spying on you," I said with a smile.

He smiled too.

"Yeah, I'm sorry. I didn't introduce myself. I am Bhoomi Sharma, daughter of Trinath Sharma."

"Good to know ma'am," he answered.

"Ma'am, huh? Oh my god, man! You can call me by my name, please. You can honor my father, not me. We're the same age and we can be friends," I said.

With a puzzled voice he said alright.

"So, what do you do Sameer?" I asked.

"I am in my third year of B.Sc. Maths at Andhra University," he answered.

"Okay," I said. He was sitting quite.

"Hello Boss...! should I only be the one asking all the questions or what? Don't you want to know anything about me?" I asked.

"Not like that Bhoomi, but," he murmured.

"I understand your problem but don't worry. I won't tell my dad," I replied and laughed. He smiled too.

"I'm doing my first year B.Com (Hon) at Andhra University too. As you are senior to me, are you going to rag me in the college?" I asked.

"Who's going to dare to rag you? No one," Sameer said.

"It's all right, I was just kidding. So if you have any issues with anyone in college, you can tell me. I'm going to see their end," I said.

"No, I don't have any issues with anybody. But thank you for your concern," he answered.

"The rain has stopped. I'm leaving now. Thank you for your company and pleasure meeting you," he said.

I said bye and came inside. I was just amazed at his innocence.

'Sirimalle Puvva' is a song from the movie *'Padaharella Vayasu'*, it was playing on the radio. I love to listen to the songs on the radio. I didn't know what happened to me but I had lost my control after meeting Sameer. I had lost my mind. I couldn't concentrate on

anything. I just loved his remembrance. I guess I fell for him.

Yet how could have I fallen for him in just one meeting? Was I too quick to act like that? But Laila Majnu and Paru Devdas both fell in love at first sight and we regard them as the best lovers. So I didn't think I was wrong in my decision. I just really loved this guy and needed to communicate this to him as soon as I could.

After I got that I was in love, every little thing made me happy. I was just grateful for everything. I was smiling more than I did before. It was all because of Sameer although he didn't do anything to me. In fact, we spoke very little but I was just impressed looking at him when he had entered our house on his scooter.

University Campus

Every vehicle and every student was stopped for a while because of a white ambassador that had entered the campus. It belonged to Trinath Sharma and dropped me and picked me up from campus every day. Everybody was scared of my dad. So they made way for me first and nobody dared to make eye contact with me which I hated the most. I was not enjoying that life, I felt I didn't have freedom to speak to my friends because of the tight security. If the same situation continued, I knew I wouldn't be able to talk to Sameer on campus. He came to my home accidentally but I never knew then that we were going to meet at my home again. So, I decided to talk to my dad to get rid of the security and demanded I should be allowed to come to college in a rickshaw.

I stepped out of the car and started walking to my classroom. I called a random guy in the corridor and he was scared to come to me. I called him again and told him that nobody would hurt him.

"Ma'am, tell me," he asked with a shivering voice.

"Hey, relax, why are you scared to talk to me? Don't worry about it. I just need the route to the 3rd year of B.Sc class," I said.

"Ma'am, it's on the first floor, the second room on the left," he replied.

"Ok, thank you," I replied and went to my class room. I attended all of my classes and went to the first floor to meet Sameer in the lunch hour.

While I was climbing the stairs, everybody was making way for me to the next floor and when I walked into Sameer's classroom, everyone in the classroom came out. In the corner bench, Sameer was writing notes. He immediately stood up after realizing that I had entered the classroom.

"Hello.. Ma'aaamm… sorry, sorry... yeah, Bhoomi! What are you doing here? This isn't your classroom," he said in a vague tone.

"Hey, Relax man, I know this isn't my classroom. I just came here to visit you. Did you have lunch?" I asked him.

"No, not yet, I'll have it later," he said.

"Let's go! Join me for lunch from today onwards," I said.

"No, Bhoomi, I'm not going to join you, please don't trouble me here. See, all my classmates went out because you're here. If we both have lunch together, then they're going to stop talking to me too," he said.

"Oh, is that so? Are you asking me to leave your class? Okay, see what I'm going to do tomorrow. I'm going to get my dad and will complain about you that you are teasing me," I said.

"No, no. Don't do that to me, Bhoomi. Your father will kill me for sure. I'm just requesting you, not teasing. Please understand," he begged me not to talk to my dad.

"Hey, you Idiot, I'm just kidding! Why would I complain to dad about you? In fact, from tomorrow, I'm going to come in a rickshaw and has asked dad to remove all this protection around me," I told. "See, no junior girl is coming to the senior class and asking the senior to join her for lunch, which I'm doing for you even though I'm Trinadh Sharma's daughter. Don't you get why I'm doing that?" I asked.

"I don't get it but it's causing me more anxiety. Why did you start talking to me? If anyone complains about this to my dad or your dad, then I'm gone," he said.

"Don't worry, who will dare to tell them this? No one's got that gut," I answered. "Sameer, I'm hungry, please let us go to the canteen and have something," I begged.

"Yet I accept that on one condition. If you agree, then I will join you," he said.

"My God, man! Are you keeping conditions for me? Well, what is it?" I asked.

"I will directly come to the canteen every day, so please don't come to my classroom," he said.

"Ok, hmm. It's agreed...! Let's just go for now," I said.

"You go first, I'm going to follow you in a distance," he said. I agreed and came out of the classroom. Poor classmates of Sameer! They were waiting for me to come out.

I got down from the first floor and Sameer followed me in a distance. I enjoyed it. I assumed that my long hair and curved hips could at least be seen by Sameer from the back. But I don't think that innocent fool had observed.

We reached the canteen and I got my box from home which had already been arranged by my guards on a table. I asked them to leave the canteen. As soon as they left, Sameer came with the Dal rice dish that the canteen was serving.

"Hey, Sameer, we both can share my lunch. It's got all sorts of non-veg curries, I can't complete all of them. Give that plate to another student. Please have this stuff," I said.

"No, Bhoomi, if I get addicted to tasty food, my family and my status won't be able to afford it later. So don't force me to eat that food. I'm comfortable with this," he said.

"Okay, I'm going to have the same food which you are having from today onwards," I said.

"That's not right Bhoomi, you've got all the facilities and good food, why will you have this poor's food? Please don't do that," he said.

"If you're happy with that food then I'll have that too,' I said.

"Your wish Bhoomi, I can't force you to do anything," he said.

I gave all my food to the other students and I also took Dal rice from the canteen. Me and Sameer both had food sitting together.

I mean, really, the food sucked. It wasn't good at all. I managed to eat it in front of Sameer but I felt like vomiting later and it hurt my stomach as well.

The Proposal

It took nearly two months for me to persuade my father to allow me to ride in a rickshaw to the college without any security. He first said no to it and every day he sent security to the college with me. Every day I fought with my dad to get rid of it and eventually he accepted it.

Me and Sameer started having food together every day at lunch time. One of Sameer's friends, Girish also started joining us but with fear. I assured him that he would not be hurt by anyone.

I had been thinking of telling Sameer about my feelings from last week, but was afraid to lose him. He was scared of my father, moreover his father worked with my father. He was afraid of his father too. I didn't dare to express my feelings directly but if I didn't, his education would be over in the near future and he will leave college soon. It would be very difficult later because I won't find another opportunity to meet him.

I wanted to express my emotions in a very different way and I wanted it to be a completely different proposal that has never before been conveyed to anybody in history.

I started thinking about different ideas, keeping it in my mind. I had an issue there; I couldn't talk about it to my friends. If I spoke to them, they'd share some ideas, but I couldn't take that chance then because I knew my father's ways.

I was riding in a rickshaw alone for the first time since my birth that day. I sounded like a bird being set free from a cage. I felt free then, I could talk to anyone I wanted. Nobody in the city knew that I was Trinath Sharma's daughter.

It is always a very happy feeling to be independent. These many days I had missed that feeling. I believe that after Sameer came into my life, I dared to speak to my father for my freedom. If one meeting in my life could bring these many changes, how wonderful it could be if we got married and lived together? I didn't want to miss him.

'Sister, your college has arrived," said the rickshaw puller.

Yeah, I had lost my mind over Sameer and I hadn't realized that my college had arrived. I got down from the rickshaw and gave him a rupee and I started walking to the college.

"Sister... Sister... Take your 80 Paisa change," shouted rickshaw guy.

I had never traveled in any private vehicle other than our own cars. I didn't know anything about the rates. I just grinned at him, took the change and went back to college. That guy was an honest man, otherwise it would have been very easy for him to cheat me and take the money. I attended the first period, but there was only one thing in my mind- how to propose? Then one thought struck me, it was to engrave our names on a tree and show it to Sameer. I thought it was the best idea ever.

Once the class was over, I left the campus and went to my favorite place on the top of the hill. My dad used to bring me there for a picnic from my childhood. When I was five years old, I had planted a tree there on my birthday and now it has grown very big. So I decided to engrave our name on it and I wanted to show it to him.

With great difficulty, I etched our names. After seeing "Bhoomi Loves Sameer" on the tree, I felt very happy. I just hugged the tree and kissed it where I had drawn our names. Right from there, I went home with a lot of joy awaiting for the next day.

My dad was sitting in the verandah and seeing me he asked me about my security-free experience. I kissed my father and thanked him for giving me such a happy life.

He smiled and said, "Whatever my daughter wants, I'm sure I'll give it to her. I'm not going to disappoint her."

With his comment, I had faith that, once everything was resolved, I could tell him about Sameer.

'Still, baby, I'm giving you freedom because I know you're not going to let my pride down. And whatever you want, you have all the right to ask me. I don't want any third-person interference between us, do you have my point?" he asked.

"Yes father, you've given me all the freedom from my childhood and I promise that in the future, I myself, will ask you whatever I want," I said and went inside.

I had arranged everything for the next day's proposal and my father also had given me such independence that once Sameer accepts, I would tell my father as well. Moin uncle is very close to my father, and I had been seeing him since childhood. My father respects Moin uncle the most. When he gets to know that I love the son of Moin uncle, he would readily accept our marriage. I fell asleep with that happy thought in my head.

I woke up early in the morning. If you're very happy and waiting for something awesome to happen, your unconscious mind is also going to be involved and makes you get up long before you want to get up.

I got ready and started for college earlier than normal.

"Dear... why are you going to college so early today?" Dad questioned.

"Dad, I've got a special class today, so I'm leaving early," I replied.

"Okay, I'll ask the driver to drop you off at college, then," he said.

"No dad, I'm going to manage in the rickshaw," I replied.

"Are you sure of that?" he asked.

"Sure dad, don't worry," I said and I started.

No student had yet arrived by the time I had entered the college, waiting for Sameer sitting on the stairs. Few of my classmates came and my friends asked me why

I came early and sat on the stairs, but I scolded them not to ask anything, as I had a lot of tension.

"Sister, why are you sitting here? Are you waiting for Sameer? He was also searching for you yesterday, where were you?" Girish asked.

The man who knows all about me and Sameer is Girish. I smiled at him and I said, "Bro, you just leave from here. I'm not waiting for anyone to arrive."

From the inside I was very glad that he was looking for me.

"Hey, I know it sister, don't worry, he's going to be at the campus in ten minutes," he said and he left smiling.

After learning that he was coming in ten minutes, my pulse doubled and I could hear my heartbeat clearly. Then he entered the campus through the gate on his scooter. His hair was flowing in slow motion and I could only focus on him. I couldn't take my eyes off of him. He parked his vehicle, got down and with his left hand, he fixed his hair and walked towards me.

"Oh, Bhoomi, what a surprise, huh? A big shots' daughter like you comes to college on time, too? And can leave college early without anyone's notice? Is that it?

Where were you yesterday and how did you come early today?" he asked.

I know he teases me, but I truly enjoyed it. If it was another guy in his place, he would have died in my hands.

"Yeah. Generally speaking, I rarely come in time, but this is a special day for me. So I came and waited for you. And do I need your permission to get out of here? Huh?" I replied.

"My permission, huh? Not needed at all, it's alright, but why wait for me? We meet at lunch, don't we? Is it your birthday today?" he asked.

"Yeah, we're going to having lunch together, but it's different from a regular day or my birthday. Can we just go to another place? I'm going to tell you why I was waiting for you. Can you drive me there, please?" I asked.

"Now, huh? No way, I've got classes. Please, let's go in the evening," he said.

"I've been waiting for you here since morning and now you're refusing to come along with me. That's just how much you owe me importance? If you miss a day of class, what are you going to lose? Am I not more important than the class?" I asked.

"Not like that, but classes are important, right? Okay! Okay! Let's go, if I talk like that you're not going to let me go to the class or you're not going to go. Here they're all just staring at us. Now better off leaving the place," he said and started walking in the direction of his scooter. I jumped with joy and we began to get to the tree where I had etched our names.

"Hey, Bhoomi, what's this place? Why did you get me here?" he asked.

"Sameer, I don't know how to tell this and how you're going to react after I tell you. But I don't have any other choice now. If I'm late, you're going to leave the campus shortly then I'm not going to be able to meet you again," I said. Confused, he gave me a strange look.

"What the hell are you talking about Bhoomi? Have you lost your mind? You got me here to this hill and now you're talking all this shit," he said.

"See Sameer, this isn't shit. I just wanted to share all my feelings with you. I've just etched my feelings on that tree, just see it," I showed him the carving.

He held his waist with one hand and after seeing it closed his mouth with the other hand in shock.

Sigh.. "What is that Bhoomi? Somehow you lost your mind. Was there any hint or actions I gave to motivate you to love me? If yes, I am sorry. It was my mistake to be a friend to you," he told.

"What went wrong? Sameer, I love you, it's a pure feeling. Why are you acting like this? Actually when you came to my home to drop your dad, I fell in love with you at first sight. I came to your class only to start talking to you," I said.

"How do you think a very poor and common man will love you and moreover the son of your father's servant? Is it possible Bhoomi? It will never happen. Now don't pressure me and let us go, I will drop you at the college," he said.

"What's wrong in that Sameer? Is it your mistake that you're not rich? Or mine that I was born into a wealthy family? Love is a pure feeling that will thrive in your heart and will not see money, caste or religion of the other person," I told.

"Whatever you say Bhoomi, I don't have any feelings for you. It won't happen. Let's go, please," he said.

"Sameer, you are hurting my feelings. And you don't know me, I will die if you don't accept that," I said.

"Please don't act like an immature person, Bhoomi. You know all our boundaries and it won't happen. Please understand and get on the scooter, I'm going to drop you in the college," he said.

"Okay... You don't love me right? I don't want your support here. I know how to go home from here. I'm going to go home later. Please leave," I said crying.

"You crazy girl! Please come, I'm going to drop you. Please, don't be dumb," he requested.

"Sameer, take your words back. You have no right to call me dumb or crazy. You still see my money in me, you have to act like a servant and survivors don't call their boss this way," I scolded.

"Oh my god—! You have gone nuts! All right, Ma'am, last time I'm begging you, please come, I will drop you. Otherwise," he said, "I'll leave."

"Leave? Whom are you threatening?" I said.

"All right. I'm going," he said and he went away.

I cried a lot because I had never faced with rejection in my life. I was not in a position to digest it. I was able to control my scream. After some time, I went home.

Trinath Sharma's Anger

After Sameer's refusal, I stopped going to college, walked out of my home, did not engage with my dad and avoided food as many times as possible. I had become very quiet and my dad was upset about my actions, he had never seen me behaving like that before.

"Dear, what happened? Why aren't you going to college? Why are you so dull? Why aren't you having food? Were you mocked by anyone in your college? Is there any problem with your teachers? Tell me, beta, why aren't you talking to me?" he kept firing questions one after the other at me.

"Nothing happened Daddy. Please don't ask me anything about that now. Please leave me alone in my room," I requested.

"Are you mad, huh? Obviously, your behavior has changed and now you're not answering my questions. In addition, you are asking me to leave the room. If you're not going to tell me what happened to you, how can I solve your problem?" dad yelled.

"Dad, I told you I remember nothing has happened to me. I'm all right. I'm going to be okay at some point. Please, just leave me alone," I begged.

"Yeah okay, then. I know how to deal with this case," he said and left. I cried a lot again after my dad left.

Dad was screaming on the phone and I could hear the sound till my bedroom.

"Moin, you're going to get the principal of college right now. I don't understand why Bhoomi is behaving like this. If required, get all students too. We've got to check if someone teased her," dad said.

After knowing that my dad had called the principal and students, I got scared. It was going to be known to everyone then. And it was not good for the future, but I was helpless.

Dad called all the maids and began to interrogate them.

"Idiots, Bhoomi hasn't had food for the past few days and she hasn't gone to college. Why didn't you inform me? You think I won't know what's going on at home?"

"Not like that sir, we asked Bhoomi ma'am to have food a few times but she scolded us. So we didn't understand what to do either. We were scared to tell you, sir," they said.

"Is there any change you've seen in her for a few days?" dad asked.

"No sir, we haven't seen anything. She was as jovial as she was with us before," they responded.

"What happened, then? Why this change all of a sudden? Why wouldn't she have food? Why wouldn't she attend college too soon after she started going to college without security? Did the rickshaw guy misbehave with her?"

"Ranga... get that rickshaw wala too! We shouldn't miss anybody here. If I can't make my daughter happy, then why all this wealth and strength," dad said.

After dad's actions, I got more scared and with my stupid behavior, these many people were going to suffer regardless of any mistakes. I was totally a fool. I wasn't supposed to behave like this. But how can I persuade Sameer and let him know how much I love him?

In the meantime, Moin uncle came to my home with my principal and all the students. There was Sameer as well in the crowd.

Principal greeted my dad and my dad was already mad. So, he kept staring at him.

"Sir, what happened? You told us to come here all of a sudden. Was there a mistake we made, sir?" principal asked him quietly.

"How many days has it been since my daughter came to college?" Dad asked.

"It's been a week, sir," he responded.

'Then, why didn't you tell me she wasn't attending the college? What happened in college, huh? Why wouldn't she attend classes? Did any of you taunt her?" he screamed at the students.

"Sir, I thought that there was some kind of function at home, I'm sorry. No one dares to speak to her, so how would they taunt her?" the principal responded.

"Hey Moin, in the group your son is also there, right? Ask him if he knows anything about it," dad asked Moin Uncle.

Huh! After listening to Sameer's name, my heart beat faster. I was afraid if Sameer would tell my dad anything about us. If so, he would kill me. I was done then.

"Sameer, come over here. Do you know what happened to Bhoomi in college? She has been really upset for a couple of days, she wouldn't have her meals and doesn't get out of her room," Moin Uncle said.

"I don't know exactly what happened, but I know that she hasn't been to college for a couple of days. As you work here, she just talks to me in college, so I knew that she was not attending college. The students don't know anything, please let them go," Sameer said.

"Sameer, as she's a friend of yours, why don't you try to talk to her once and sort out the problem," my dad said.

Meanwhile, Ranga came with the rickshaw puller. My dad stood up from the chair and slapped his face.

"You son of a bitch! You just drove my daughter to college. Did you tease her?" he yelled.

The rickshaw puller fell on my dad's feet and started crying, "Sir, I did nothing. I took the utmost care while driving sister."

"Sir, don't hurt him. I'm going to talk to Bhoomi and figure it out. Please let everyone leave," Sameer asked.

"All right," dad agreed.

Sameer came to my room.

"Hi Bhoomi, what's going on here? Why are you doing all this stuff? Have you gone mad? See how many people are suffering because of you. Please, enough of this. Stop all these and come to college from tomorrow," he whispered.

"Oh, no matter whatever I say or do, every time I am wrong, and you have every right to reject my proposal, and you can leave me alone. Waaaaah Sameer sir! What kind of logic! And my studies is my wish and my health, my wish. Let them suffer, what can I do?" I answered.

"I didn't mean you were wrong, but your action isn't right. If I have done any wrong, you can punish me but not yourself and others. I can't love you, why don't you get that? Please don't do all of this. I'm asking you to agree to have food properly and come to class. Rest we will talk in the college," he said.

"No, I will not accept any of your requests until you accept my love. When I hurt myself, why are you worried about me? If it worries you, it means that you love me, too," I argued.

"You crazy girl, why don't you get it? I can't love you. If I love you, your dad's going to kill my entire family, just let it go. Please have food," he pleaded.

"Come here, sit down here," I asked. He came and sat in front of me on the ground.

"Please don't do this, please accept. We will talk about everything in college. Here, I can't explain you everything, understand?" he started begging me.

"Sameer, look into my eyes. How badly is it swollen? Do you think any girl is going to cry like this for you?" I asked.

'No, Bhoomi, that's what my problem is. I don't want any girl to suffer because of me, especially you," he said.

I was going mad and I didn't understand how to express my love to him. No matter what happened later, I was ready to face it. I kissed his lips and said, "You fool I love you, don't you understand?" I cried. He was sitting silently, unable to respond in the shock.

"Sameer, what happened to you? Why are you silent?" I asked.

He just grabbed my head and kissed me back and said, "I love you, too, let us face whatever happens later.

Now you eat food and come to college tomorrow," he said and left.

For a moment, I was surprised and pleased. I was happier and happier. I couldn't even say how pleased I was. After a change in my actions and attitude, my father was also happy. After that, my father allowed Sameer to come to my home and visit me.

The Arrangements

Every year my father celebrates the wedding event of Rama and Sita with a very grand gathering for Sri Rama Navami. That year as usual the preparation for it began. I and Sameer were very happy that time as we had been in love for quite some time and we both felt every pinch of love in our life.

Like every year, our family offered a new pair of silk saree and dhoti to the lord. After the wedding celebration, we arrange a lunch for the people of our colony. Everyone was busy sorting all the stuff from the past week. They decorated the temple and the lane with bulbs and set the stage with palm tree leaves. It was a massive arrangement for all the people of the colony to sit down and see the celebration.

Sameer was busy too, making plans with Moin Uncle. He came home for one thing or the other. Every time he came, I took him to my room and we kissed. I didn't want to miss any opportunity because no one was at home, everyone was busy making arrangements at the temple. It was so fascinating that even after kissing so many times, we couldn't satisfy our desire. I didn't know whether Sameer really had work at our home or if he was coming here to kiss me, either way it felt good.

"Dear, why do you only come to pick from here where there are so many people and that too, those who work here?" I asked.

"I'm a young man who can handle multiple tasks at a time, so they're sending me here," he said.

"Yeah, you're right, I know all the multiple tasks you've been doing since morning," I said smiling.

He just winked his eye at me.

"Hey, you can't taunt Mr. Trinath Sharma's daughter. If he gets to know about it, then you're gone," I said.

"Do you know something? He's just my uncle and I have every right to do whatever I want with his daughter," he said tauntingly.

"Oh, Acha! If you have those rights, then I have the right to kill you if you misbehave with me," I said.

"Chalo — Kill me with your embrace now," he said. He came close to me and pulled me to his side holding my waist.

"Hey, leave me, don't do this. I'm tired from morning with all of these. Someone might come, please leave now," I said.

"You said you were going to kill me if I did this," he teased.

"Hey, I'm going to kill you whenever I want. Your life is in my hands now, beware of me," I taunted.

"All right, but what are you going to buy me from feast tomorrow?" I asked.

"Whatever you want, I will try to buy it for you," he responded.

"Okay then, I want green colored bangles and you have to give me a gift tomorrow at the gathering," I said.

"Oh, your dad and all his people are going to be around you tomorrow, how can that be possible? It's going to be very risky," he said.

"Can't you take some kind of risk for me?" I asked.

Sigh! "I can take it, but there's going to be a crowd, that's what I'm worried about," he said.

"I know you're scared of my dad. I'm challenging you, you can't do it tomorrow," I teased him. He stared at me.

"Sameer, what happened to you? Stop staring at me and react," I said.

"Okay Challenge accepted, if I finish the mission, what are you going to give me?" he asked.

"What do you want?" I asked in a husky voice.

"Nothing much, just your happiness, that's enough for me," Sameer said.

"Yes, my sweetie, I love you." I hugged him and kissed him on the chest.

"Okay Love, it's already late, I will leave now. We will meet there tomorrow," he said and left.

Sri Rama Navami

The house was all decorated with mango leaves and marigold flowers. All of our maids and dad's followers wore new clothes. Everyone looked amazing in white clothes.

I took a head bath in *Soapberry Water* and dried my hair with *Samrani*. I wore a new half saree for the event and went to the Pooja Room in the house. My dad was already performing pooja. I received the blessings of God and my father. I prayed to my mother.

My mother had left us when I was born and then my father took care of me. My father didn't give me a chance to miss my mother.

I wanted to go before my father left for the temple.

"Daddy, I'm going to the temple," I said.

"Bhoomi, why are you in a hurry? I'm just going there too. Wait for a while," he responded.

"No, Father, I'd like to go and see the cooking arrangements and stroll through the fair for a while. When I come with you, you're not going to let me go anywhere.

I'm going to complete my roaming by the time you come," I said.

He sighed, "You never listen to me. Alright, take care of yourself," he said. I hugged my dad and thanked him and started to the temple.

The temple was well decorated with different flowers and it spread positivity. Devotional songs were played in the mic set. The entire crowd was gathering for the celebration. I just walked into the cooking area where they were preparing a lot of food. Almost everyone was rushing to finish the work quickly, so that they could join the event as well.

The place was completely filled with smoke, so I just grabbed a carrot out of the basket and walked out of the room. I entered the temple, offered my prayers and came out and sat down at the tables arranged for everyone to gather.

I thought Sameer had been working there till morning, which was why both Moin uncle and Sameer weren't available there. He didn't know that I was going to come this early to the temple, otherwise, he'd have reached here by that time. And today he had a surprise from me that I was wearing a Half Saree. I wore it to surprise him and make my love happy.

It was around 9:00 AM and the priests were announcing to gather as the event was to begin in a short time. All the children were playing around and their parents were chasing them. They announced that my father had also arrived at the venue after which I could sense the different atmosphere there all of a sudden. Everyone was silent and stood up for his entry. My father walked into the hall with Moin Uncle and Sameer accompanying him.

My father wished everybody and he told everyone to settle down. He came over and sat next to me. Sameer wore white Kurta Pyjama, looking too cute and I felt like I would jump and bite him. But I scolded my stupid mind and reminded myself that we were all sitting in a temple where we had to evade such thoughts.

They were all seated behind us, and the event began. We offered the clothes we got for the Lord. The marriage event happened in a splendid way. Each of us received the blessings of Lord Rama and Sita. I asked God to give blessings to get married to Sameer by the next Sri Rama Navami. I hoped he granted my wish without any obstacles.

We all gathered for lunch after the event. Lunch was served with more than 10 items in a banana leaf. I chose to serve the dessert because no hard work was needed to serve it.

Me and Sameer moved in the opposite direction while serving. He said that I looked amazing in half a saree while crossing each other, and I replied, "it's for you only," and he just said, "thank you."

I asked him about the challenge. He asked me to come to the cooking area where all the foodstuffs were kept for those who served. I went there and he took out a box from his pocket and put it in my sweet cup. I looked around to check if someone saw it or not, but they were all busy serving food.

"Hmm... You did it man! You won the challenge!" I said and went to the place of lunch.

College Election

The college announced elections and all the unions were getting ready for the polls. Each time Sameer helped a union, it won the race. But the Party leader Jagadeesh was a senseless fellow who had done nothing for the campus. So this time everyone was against him but Sameer still continued to follow him.

As few friends of Sameer knew me, they approached me to speak to Sameer about contesting against Jagadeesh in the election. I was surprised to hear their request. Why did they ask me to speak to Sameer instead of them speak to him directly? I only asked them the same out of curiosity.

"Bhoomi, you've known him for a couple of days but he's been our friend for 3 years and he's never bothered with elections. He doesn't want to be in the race. He only supports Jagadeesh blindly although he tries to speak to Jagadeesh about the rights of students. Jagadeesh's father works for your father where Sameer's father reports to him. So he's not going to go against him. We tried to ask him to contest in the last year election but he refused," they replied.

Upon learning all these, I realized why he just didn't want to disrupt his father's workplace and I kept looking at all the mistakes of Jagadeesh. I had agreed to speak to Sameer about contesting in the next election. And if anything happens, I would take my father's help to turn the election a victory for Sameer. I had assured them this. They were happy to hear my response. They thanked me and left.

That same evening Sameer and I met on the terrace of the college. The climate was very romantic with a slight drizzle showering different flowery plants in the college lawn. The breeze spread fragrance in the air that gave freshness.

"Hey Bhoomi, Wassup my dear? You look beautiful in this light pink churidar," Sameer said. I thanked him, smiling. He praises me every day, every time we meet.

I said, "You look handsome too dear in this Denim Jacket." He smiled.

"Wah... wah... Oh My God, I only fell for you for this charming smile. I just want to kiss you now, but I missed the opportunity because it's a campus," I said.

"Oops, so I missed that too. Shit!" he said with disappointment.

"Sure, don't worry, I'm going to give you a big hug and a kiss now if you accept something I'm asking you to do," I said.

"Oh, Is it? What is it? Have you come up with a plan here then? Huh?" he asked.

"If you agree to the condition, I will tell you," I said.

"I am the fool or what to miss a girl's hug and kiss. Whatever you want, I'm going to do it for you," he answered.

"All right then, you have promised me that you will do it," I said and kissed his cheek and hugged him. I made my line clear for asking him to contest in the election. And that he had no chance other than contesting.

"Hey Bhoomi, you didn't tell me what to do, anyways. You've given all these to me before," he said.

"Sameer, this is a very special kiss that I gave you here on campus. I believe you're not going to break your promise, so I kissed you before asking," I replied.

"I'm not going to break it, you can ask me now dear," he said.

"I want you to be the president of the college while you are leaving campus, so I want you to contest this election against Jagadeesh," I said.

"What? What...? Me, the President? Why do you talk about politics all of a sudden? Who injected all of these into your mind? And I never wanted to be the president. I don't like all of these. I'm just here to study," he said, "Please do not push me to do it."

"Injecting? Who's going to do that to me? Anyone got guts to speak directly to me on campus? And also why don't you want to be the president? Or do you want to be a follower of Jagadeesh, that idiot? I know you're here to study, but a genuine guy like you should be right in the front line to lead all the other students in the right direction. So, you've got to compete in the race as you promised. If you're afraid of Jagadeesh or his father, don't worry. If required I 'm going to get my dad. Then nobody's going to talk," I said.

"Not Jagadeesh or his father, but I never wanted to concentrate on that. And the college is entirely the sole property of the students, we should not encourage any outsiders to enter the campus because of elections or any other support,"

"Even, I don't want to be involved, it can lead to some other situations. Every time I've been helping Jagadeesh and this time if I challenge him, he'll definitely take revenge on me. But we can do one thing, we can submit Jagadeesh with the list of demands we need, where I will be standing up for those and fighting," he said, "please accept."

"Sameer, No. I want you to be first, but you're running out of the contest? So, whatever promise you made is not authentic and you fooled me," I said.

"You've mistaken me dear, I'm still on my words. I'm going to do anything you ask me to do, but this one thing, please no," he said.

"It's all right Sameer, I 'm leaving. There's nothing you 're going to do for me, I got it. Probably, I was wrong, I believed in you. Just let it go. I got to go," I said and began to leave.

He just grabbed my hand from behind and said, "Bhoomi, if you want to see me as the college president, let's go rock the elections," he said.

With his acceptance of taking part in the elections, I turned back with a gigantic smile on my face and jumped on him hugging with joy.

"Thank you Sameer, thank you so much, I knew you would accept to take part in the elections. Now I'm very happy," I said.

"Bhoomi, I will do all that for you. I just want you to be happy. But we have a problem here," he said.

"What is it? Sameer," I asked.

"In order to participate with a new symbol in the elections, we have to sign it with the principal office and announce it to the campus. We need some fee to deposit and we need posters and flags. We need a lot of money to arrange all of these," he said.

"You don't worry about the money and arrangements, give me one day, I will arrange," I said.

"But, how? I don't understand where you are going to get money from," he was confused.

"Now don't worry about the money, I'm going to take care of it. You should just focus on your campaigning from tomorrow," I said.

"See Bhoomi, I don't want your father's money to be used in the expenses of college. Let me check with friends and make arrangements," he said.

"Hey chill Sameer, I don't even want to ask my dad. I have some savings with me and I will make some more plans with my friends. You just leave money matter to me and let's go for now. I'll meet you in college tomorrow morning and talk to the rest of the students," I said and we left.

I arrived at the college the next morning a little earlier than usual. By the time Sameer reached college, I called each and every student to gather at the ground. Everybody was worried why I was asking them to suddenly gather.

Even Jagadeesh had come to the meeting with his followers. He was puzzled too and waited for me to reveal why I had called everybody there. He couldn't even attempt to ask me.

Sameer entered the campus and the wait was over. I could see his face brimming with anxiety and surprise. He parked his vehicle and came up to me.

"Hey, what's going on here, Bhoomi?" he asked and wiped off the sweat on his brow.

"When you contest in an election, the opening is supposed to be this big, Sameer. So I just called everyone here to announce it," I said.

"What? What are you talking about, Bhoomi? Have you lost your mind or what? See Jagadeesh is here too, it will lead to a fight between our two groups," he said.

"Don't worry Sameer, nobody's going to pluck anything and Jagadeesh, the funny guy, do you think he is going to try to talk to me? You be cool and go announce it," I said.

"I don't understand this, you are messing it all up. I don't know where this is going to go," he said.

"Well then, I messed it up, right? Let me handle it and put it right," I said and went and stood on a table, which was already lying there.

"Hello! My dear college friends, thanks to everybody who has gathered irrespective of branch or group. We're gathered here to announce a great thing that many of you are hoping for and few are going to hate."

All of a sudden everyone became attentive and looked at each other's faces in surprise after listening to me.

"How many of you would like to know what I'll announce?" I asked them. Most of them raised their hands and few kept their faces blank.

"Yeah.. yes.. I just want that josh!"

"As our presidential college elections are announced, who will you elect as your President?" I asked.

"Anna Jagadeesh !!" The crowd shrieked and all of a sudden I could detect a proud smile on Jagadeesh 's face.

"Okay... Okay...... From the past two elections, he has been winning as the president and what difference did he bring to our campus?" I asked.

There was a sudden silence amongst the crowd. Jagadeesh hadn't expected that question. I could see the surprise on his face then.

"The silence clearly shows that it is the time to change our president. So I'm nominating the presidential candidate for next elections, our senior friend, Mr. Sameer. How many of you would vote for him?" I asked.

The ground blasted with double the sound than before and a few of Sameer's friends took him to the table where I stood. Jagadeesh's face suddenly grew red with anger and he left the ground.

Everybody was starting to shout "President Sameer Zindabad!" Our party symbol was revealed by Sameer which was a 'pen'.

"Friends, as we are in this election for the first time, we need some fund to submit the application as well as for the campaign. I can give 150 rupees personally for this election and I ask everyone to help and donate money to support Sameer," I said.

With that announcement, everyone immediately came forward and put the money on the table and we collected nearly 500 rupees. We thanked everyone and began our election preparation.

Days passed and Sameer's triumph could be seen clearly. Jagadeesh tried multiple times to mob our friends. I gave him the ultimate warning and he kept quiet.

The Election Day arrived and the voting began. While we stood in front of the voting hall for a status check, everyone came to Sameer and wished him all the best.

The results were out in the evening and Jagadeesh lost the election with a huge margin and Sameer won. Sameer hugged me in front of everyone with joy and the crowd started cheering.

Spoiler

We were all very happy after Sameer 's victory and we had scheduled a large gathering for the College President's oath ceremony. Me and Sameer visited the Vice-Chancellor and the Principal to invite them for the ceremony. They happily agreed to join.

Sameer's friends who had asked me to talk to Sameer for contesting in the election came to me and personally thanked me. I didn't know how it had helped them but it had helped me so much. That was the reason why my dear Sameer had become the president of the college and I and Sameer became even closer in the whole process. But there, I could not express all these to them.

We even respectfully invited Jagadeesh to the oath ceremony where he was to hand over the position he had enjoyed since the past two years. He gave us a strange look and a fake smile, as we went to him. But we couldn't help but ignore it.

That victory was celebrated by every student as their own victory, and they felt themselves as the president of their college. Everyone had worked hard to set up the stage for the oath ceremony and the remaining things.

The stage was set for the oath ceremony, students gather in the ground one by one and the guests were expected to arrive at any moment. Me and Sameer welcomed all the guests and students personally to the area of oath. Some of my mates were distributing the treats that were prepared for the ceremony of oath. The meeting we had arranged in the evening at the college. I could see the simple happiness on every student's face.

Upon the arrival of the Vice Chancellor and The Principal, we gave them some flowers, welcomed them on to the stage and felicitated the ceremony. The Vice Chancellor and the Principal appreciated Sameer and wished him the best and promised to the gathering that if there was any issue in the college campus they would provide support to each and every student to promote smooth studies and to create the best educational experience on campus.

In front of the huge gathering, Sameer made an oath and told each and every student that he would be leading the team and that he would be a point of contact for any issue raised in the campus and asked them to submit a report on whatever problems which were pending, so that he would try to close it as soon as possible.

Actually the old president needs to hand over the duties to the new one at the college oath ceremony. But Jagadeesh was not visible at the gathering. He must have been hurt, as one of his follower had become the president. But we were glad.

Once the program got successfully completed, we remained back at the college for dinner. Sameer got the pack of Mutton Biryani and Kheer from his home. The food was great.

Time was around 7.45 PM and most students had left already. Me, Sameer and some friends were still on the campus. Sameer asked his friends to leave and said that he was going to drop me off. I am simply enjoying my Kheer's last sip.

All left the campus in 10 minutes and only me and Sameer remained there.

"Thank you, Bhoomi for all that. I never thought I was going to be a college president. All this joy, this position and this respect is only because of you," he said.

"Hello Boss, don't be formal. I know how to see my boyfriend and I wanted everyone to respect you and I have been successful in that," I said.

He stood up from the spot and came to me, he hugged me with joy. I had been waiting for this moment for such a long time, the tight hug and some privacy. We had been busy campaigning since many days and had been surrounded by students and didn't get an opportunity.

"Sameer, for all the pains and gains this is medicine. Can we commit it with this happy note?" I asked him.

"Commit what?" Sameer asked.

"Nobody is around, it's surrounded by darkness, romantic weather and we're in a happy mood, nevertheless. Would we make a naughty mistake?" I asked.

"I have no problem, if you're all right to do that," Sameer said.

"You're a stupid guy seriously, why do you waste time asking all these stupid questions? I, myself am telling you to do this," I felt angry at him.

"Huh.. ok dear, but on campus? If anyone sees us, then?" he asked.

He was wasting time asking all dumb questions and I needed to do something right then.

I stood up from the chair and moved towards him, clutched his shirt's collar and pulled him towards me.

"Hey madam...! What is it that you are doing? You are clutching the college president's shirt. This isn't good for you," Sameer said, "he could hurt you."

"I was even looking for it that he can respond to me at least now," I said.

"Aha..!" he said.

I covered his mouth with my lips so as to stop him from saying another word that was wasting our time. He just followed me and started kissing me, gripping my waist and pulling closely towards him and then began kissing even harder.

He started kissing everywhere he wanted to kiss, and I was loving it. I hugged him really close as it brought me more joy. I felt very light and I felt like I was flying on the clouds.

"Come on Sameer, let's start the real game, why are you prolonging the game for too long? Please start," I said.

He pushed me away from him a little and said, "Yeah, Bhoomi, I feel this isn't the right thing we're doing right now, please let's go back home now. Your father believes you and we're not going to break his trust. Please understand me, let's go, it's already late."

After listening to his statement, I began to cry unintentionally. Not only does he take care of me, but he thinks of a father's tradition and belief. I just behaved like a fool and provoked him to do all these things.

"Thanks Sameer, for taking care of my father's trust and me. I have made no mistake in loving you, and I am proud of my choice. You are the real man and the true man who respects traditions. I love you forever and ever since. You 're the only person in my life.'

"All right, dear let's go for now."

I kissed him again and we started to go back home. Sameer dropped at my home, and he left.

As I walked into the house, I saw my father sitting outside very seriously and Moin uncle standing in front of him. I could see that all the flower pots were broken and the area was completely messed. For some time, I didn't understand, but I walked into the house in silence.

"Bhoomi....!" Dad called me out very seriously. And I had never heard him call me so bad.

He was so angry in his voice and I didn't know what made him so angry. I stopped going inside and then looked at him.

"What happened, Dad? Why are you being so serious?" I asked whispering.

"You dumb girl... you don't know what you've done? And now questioning me innocently as if you do not know anything," he shouted.

"What did happen, father? I seriously don't know. Stop shouting at me please, and tell me what happened?" I asked.

"How dare you speak this way to me," he said and slapped me. I never expected that and since my childhood he had never acted with me like that. For a moment, I was stunned and I began to cry.

"I don't know dad, seriously, what happened and why did you hit me?" I asked crying

"You know nothing, don't you? All right, now you will know all," he said and called Jagadeesh.

Jagadeesh, with a sly smile on his face, stepped out from my house.

Then I got it all, that idiot must have told my father about me and Sameer's relationship which was why Moin Uncle had to stand in front of my father with his hands folded.

"Daddy...! You believed this fool and you hit me, but I can explain it to you," I said.

"What is it that you can explain? Didn't you love Moin's son Sameer?" he shrieked.

"Yes...! I loved him and I still love him, but we were about to tell you this in a couple of weeks. But in the meantime this fool ruined everything," I glared at Jagadeesh.

"I gave you all this freedom, because I thought my daughter wouldn't cheat me. Moreover, I never expected to hear this kind of news from a dog like Jagadeesh today. I even told you that you have all the rights to tell me anything but now you've just cheated your father and killed him from inside. Don't show me your face. Ranga, cancel her college admission and lock her at home, if she leaves home I'll kill you all, understand?" he screamed.

"But Dad... when you listened to Jagadeesh and believed him, why don't you listen to me and why don't you understand what your daughter says? Don't do this to me, please, dad, I really love Sameer and he's a very nice person. I 'm sorry that I didn't updated you, but please understand our love and accept it," I grieved.

"Ranga, don't you understand what I just said? Just drag this slut out of here. I don't want to see her anymore. And Moin, I don't know what you and your son are going to do, I don't want to see you again in this town from tomorrow. As you worked closely with me until now, I'm not harming you and your family, but if it goes on again, I'm going to kill your entire family, just fuck off from here and leave the city," he shouted.

After listening to my father calling me a slut I just died from inside. I collapsed there. I didn't have a word out of my mouth and my tears shed uncontrollably out of my eyes. I thought my father was going to understand our love, but he believed all the fake things that a fool communicated and refused to trust his own daughter. So what would our future be like? Literally, I was lost and couldn't think.

I didn't know what was going to happen with me. Ranga dragged me into my room with the help of our maids and slammed the door.

Waiting for Sameer

I had been locked in the room for twenty days, I didn't even want to get out of the house. I wanted to kill myself, but there was a ray of hope that Sameer would come and take me out of this hell anytime. So, I kept waiting for him.

My father also stopped all the operations and because of my situation and absence of Moin uncle, he became very sad. Since they were both very close from their childhood and then started to work together, he was the most trusted member of my dad's squad.

I tried to speak to Ranga and told him to speak to Sameer, but he declined to do me any favor because fearing my father. I begged him, but he told me that he would not do that because he was working for us. So he couldn't help me because he had more respect for my dad.

I asked him to get Sameer's details at least on how he was doing and where he was. Finally, he agreed to try.

I checked my father's condition with him, he said' "Boss is very sad and he isn't meeting anybody. He isn't even stepping out of his room nowadays. He's skipping his meals and with that chance, Jagadeesh's father has become the most powerful. He's conducting all the operations that dad used to do."

Having learnt about my father, I felt very bad. I asked Ranga to talk to my father to give me a chance to explain and shed all this darkness from our lives. I wanted to explain that all these happened because of Jagadeesh which my father failed to understand.

All of a sudden, I heard my father called Ranga and after sometime Ranga came to me again and told me that my father was asking me to get ready as a guy was coming to see me for marriage.

"I'm going to die here, but I won't see anyone, you go and tell my father that," I shouted.

From then on he tried several times to get me ready for marriage and he stopped asking me about the marriage after a few days.

It had been three months since I had been locked away and there was no information on Sameer. I used to ask Ranga for the information every day.

Dad went to the city one day to check on some registration job and then Ranga came to me.

"Bhoomi, give me any of Sameer's friend's details, I'm going to get the information for you, but don't tell anyone that I'm helping," he said.

"I'm going to die but I'm not going to tell anyone. Thank you for helping me," I gave him some information of his friends.

I was very curious about Sameer's situation after Ranga went out to get the details. I waited for him with a lot of hope. Ranga returned but my wait was broken. There was no information that he could collect about Sameer but he had got me his address from one of our friends, Girish. I couldn't help myself but write a letter to Sameer.

I wrote a letter to Sameer with a lot of courage asking him to come and take me with him no matter whatever happened. It was posted with Ranga 's help.

I waited for Sameer's reply but I didn't receive it and I hadn't heard anything about Sameer for so long. I was disappointed, depressed and clueless about why Sameer didn't reply or come for me. I wanted to commit suicide and attempted several times but my father saved me from all my attempts.

Later, I realized how stupid I was and never tried to understand Sameer's situation. I wanted to die and blame him for everything. My father also realised my pain about love and tried to accept it but it was too late for him to tell me. I lost my father after his cardiac arrest. After that I was left alone. Due to these two tragedies, I wanted to leave the city, so I sold all my property and came to Hyderabad and started this Old age home.

I didn't marry anyone in memory of Sameer only, and was still waiting for his reply. She said wiping tears.

George's Realisation

"After listening to your story I can easily see how stupid our generation is. You are such a true lover, who still awaits him."

I broke up with Ananya recently for a stupid reason. I had liked a picture of a girl who was my friend and Ananya didn't like it and told me not to do it again, but what did I do? I fought foolishly with her and broke up. What an idiot I am, will I not compromise the little things and make my girl happy? Just then I realized the meaning of true love.

Shit, it was too late then. I had to call her then and say sorry. I got up and went out of the room and began to call her. She rejected my call. I knew she was upset with me and maybe she didn't want to talk to me, but it was my mistake, I must go through this punishment.

I was not going to give up, I called her again and she disconnected the call again. Then I sent a message through Whatsapp. She checked the message but did not respond.

'*Hi Ananya, I called you to express my sorry. Please respond or pick up my call. I realized how big mistake I made, please forgive me,*' I messaged.

I sent two crying emojis along with the message.

She checked that message too, but did not respond.

I returned to the room with great disappointment.

"What is the matter my son? Why do you look so upset," Granny asked.

"After listening to your story, I realized what's true love and called my girlfriend to apologize. As we broke up for a stupid reason recently, she didn't respond," I said.

"Don't worry, my son, she certainly will respond. We ladies take all the pain and easily forgive men. She had to wait for your call for so long, all of a sudden when you phone, she has to weep out of your missing feeling."

"It's all because of me. I just put so much pain on her. I'm supposed to be punished," I said.

"You've now realized your mistake, that's enough. No need to be punished separately," granny said.

In the meantime my phone rang and it was Ananya.

"Baby, I'm so sorry. I brought you a lot of pain. I am never going to repeat this again, please forgive me. I love you so much," I started speaking endlessly after I picked up the call.

The other side remained silent.

"Ananya what happened? Why are you so quiet? There was so much tension and questions going through my mind. I could hear some sound and it was Ananya weeping.

"Hey honey, why are you crying now? I realized my mistake and I won't hurt you again, and I will listen to whatever you say. And I'm going to delete all social media applications from my phone, I promise. At least now please smile," I asked.

"Where had you been these days? You needed these many days to realise or what? Do you know how much I was crying these days? You jerk, don't ever do that to me again," she said.

"No. No. I promise I will never do this. I love you baby, sorry for everything. Smile at least now," I said.

"You idiot," she said smiling.

After listening to her smile, I felt very happy. I felt like I had won the battle and I was the king of the world. That's the power of love.

"Where are you?" she asked.

"Hey, Honey, there's a lovely person you need to meet. Can you come straight to Begumpet? Me and Joseph are here only. I will send you the map location," I said.

"Why? And what are you people doing there? I 'm working now, I'm not going to meet anyone, you carry on," she said.

"Hey, it's a chance to meet these people. I can't explain everything over the phone, you come here and you're coming, that's it," I said.

"Alright, give me some time to get there," she said.

I said well and disconnected the phone.

Ananya reached the old-age home after an hour. I introduced Ananya to Bhoomi and told Bhoomi's story and all that happened those days. Ananya also felt very happy to meet Bhoomi.

There was still silence and unhappiness inside me. Because I was not satisfied, the wallet and the letter were the reasons behind the whole thing that happened. We did whatever we could but couldn't find Mr. Sameer. But the best thing in my life was knowing their great story, and meeting Bhoomi.

We told Bhoomi our last goodbye and started leaving the old age home.

Bhoomi called me, "Son, take with you this letter, I don't need it," she gave me the letter.

"No, granny, this is your love's memory, you keep it with you. It'll make you feel a little better," I said.

"The letter is Sameer's own. I expressed everything I needed and waited for the response. I feel the message hasn't reached the person if I keep this back with me. A plan of god's must be behind it, otherwise why does it come to you and why did you come so long to know the reason behind it. So I don't want to interrupt it," she said, "let it travel until I get my answer."

Could be... maybe that's the reason.

I said okay and took back the letter and kept it in the wallet. With Bhoomi 's blessings, we came out of her room.

The Watchman

As I came out, I decided to hand over the wallet to the old age home watchman so that, as Bhoomi believes, it will travel until she gets the answer to her letter and the guy who helped me can use the amount in the wallet. I thanked him for his support, gave him the wallet and asked him to take the money.

Everything between us three was very silent. We were disappointed about why the two beautiful souls were separated by God? Bhoomi's father should at least have listened to her once. So many thoughts ran in our minds.

We started our bikes without even talking to each other because nobody was in the mood to talk. And suddenly the watchman came running over to us.

Breathing heavily he said, "Sir..! Where did you find the wallet?" he asked.

"Hey... calm down dude..! What went wrong? Are you not happy with the amount in the wallet? Need something more?" I asked.

"Sir, this is not about money, it's about the wallet. And this wallet belongs to our professor. This is not for the first time he lost it, but so many times. Whenever someone gets this wallet he usually wants to meet and thank them personally. So I came here to take all of you to him," he said.

What…? what..?!!

I, Joseph and Ananya looked at each other's faces and saw a spark of happiness in our eyes.

"Oh my god, man...! Are you serious? Is it your professor? Really? Or are you kidding?" I asked him surprised.

"I'm serious, I 'm sure it's Sameer sir's wallet," he said, "Lets go."

I just jumped from the bike and picked him up, and danced with joy.

'Saab, saab, Neeche utaro.. kyathobhi pagal hain bhai tu..'

In Hyderabadi Hindi, he started shouting to get him down and called me crazy.

Yeah, it happened as Bhoomi said, that it could be God's game and that he uses us as his messengers. And see the magic, both of them were staying at the same old-age home without knowing each other. God has got to be crazy.

We parked our bikes and without wasting a single minute, entered the old age home again but this time the male block.

When we were taken inside by the watchman, Sameer didn't know we were coming, he was sitting on the armchair, reading a book.

"Sir," watchman called him.

"Yeah.. Who?" he asked while adjusting his spectacles.

He was still very handsome and fit for his age. He wore a white pajama kurta and looked stunning.

"What Rudrayya? Who are these youngsters? Why did you bring them down here?" he asked in English.

"This time these gentlemen got your wallet sir," he replied.

"Oh.. Is it? Thanks boys, there's an old memory in it that doesn't go away from me. I've lost it several times, but it's coming back to me again and again," he said.

"Why sir? You don't want that memory to stay with you or what? Do you dislike them the most?" I asked.

"Come on, come here and sit down. Rudrayya, get us all some coffee," he said.

We went there, and sat down.

"Hmmm… That memory is from nearly 38 years ago and I couldn't answer that. It still squeezes me inside. I was helpless and a loser who didn't answer, so when I see that, I feel bad," he said.

"I'm sorry to say I've read your letter, Sir," I told him.

"No problem my son, now if someone reads it or not, it's not going to be of help to anyone. Those opportunities and days have passed," he said.

"But there is so much pain and love that has been expressed in it, why have you not replied Sir?" I asked.

"It is a very long story," he said.

"No problem sir, we 're going to listen, please let us know," we said.

He showed us a photograph of a girl who must be around 8 years old in the picture.

"She is the beautiful Bhoomi Sharma. I saw her for the very first time at a celebration of Sri Rama Navami in our village at a very young age. My father used to work for her father, so I go to see her frequently at their home. Whenever Mutton Biryani and Kheer was cooked by my mother, I used to give them a parcel as she doesn't have a mum. Especially in the holy month of Ramadan I used to carry a parcel of Biryani and Kheer for her."

Young Sameer

"Sameer, get up *beta,* it raining heavily and I need to report to Sharma as soon as possible because we have to go for a settlement," my dad shouted.

I jumped out of my bed, as it was a chance to see my girl again. So I quickly got ready and started off to Bhoomi's house.

As my dad was late due to the rain, one of my dad's colleagues was waiting for my dad at the gate. We just got into the house. Wah.. the rain! And a lovely melody song on the radio and a lovely girl sitting in the hall, I just came to see her and was glad to see her.

I have seen her several times before but she looked even more stunning that day. I dropped my father and waited at Bhoomi's place until it stopped raining. I was already drenched but chose to wait because I would be able to see her for a while.

Their maid offered me a cup of tea, and she told me that Bhoomi had asked her to give me tea. I thanked her and I think she noticed me for the first time and offered me a tea.

Once everyone left, she came out and sat in her dad's chair in front of me. And this was the first time she talked to me that day. And that was the day I had been waiting for, but I kept quiet as if I didn't know her.

We spoke for some time and I left for my home after the rain had stopped.

"Where have you been till now, Sameer?" my mother yelled, "Rain stopped long back."

"I went to drop my dad, ma," I replied.

"Beta, don't be too clever. I know you've been to drop pappa, but what have you been doing so far?" mom asked.

"I was just waiting there till it stopped raining," I said.

"Aha..! So you were waiting for the rain to stop, now I've to believe it?" my mother asked me holding my hair.

"Haa, Maa. It's paining, please leave my hair, yeah, I've been waiting for the rain to stop," I told her.

"Have you not waited there to see the love of your childhood?" she scolded.

Don't be shocked, my mother already knew everything, otherwise why would she give parcels of food from my childhood.

"No ma, I just waited there because of the rain," I told.

"I know you stupid, don't fool me. Okay, change your clothes," she said.

I said alright and went into my room.

"But maa, today she was so beautiful," I shouted from my room.

"If her dad gets to know about your acts, then you're gone. Be careful," she warned.

"Don't worry, Ma, I'm going to take care of it," I said.

I used to follow her car every day, which she didn't know. I used to keep every information of her and no one dared to speak to her or taunt her in college. I never tried to talk to her, either, because I too didn't know how she was going to react, but after yesterday's meeting, I realized that she was talking politely and she had a very nice tone.

Still, I didn't dare to speak to her again because if any of her guards found out, it was going to be a problem.

Suddenly, there was a disturbance in my classroom and whoever were sitting in my class were running out. I didn't know why they were rushing, but later realized that Bhoomi was coming to my class. She was not allowed to enter the seniors' classroom as a junior, but nobody could deter her there.

She came and asked me to come along for lunch with her. From inside, I was very pleased because only she spoke to me on campus and I felt special. On the other hand, I was in panic. If any of her guards told her father, then he was going to kill me.

I asked her to go and wait in the canteen, and after some time, I followed her. And then she told me she would ask her father to remove the guards and she would come to college in a rickshaw. How exciting was that? There would be no need to be in fear then because if there was no guard, we could spend time freely. I was delighted to hear that.

So, gradually we started spending our lunch hours together and she got very close to me. We used to talk on the terrace of the college and I used to drop her at her house.

Holy Ramadan

It was the month of Holy Ramadan in which I spent the whole month fasting and attending prayers five times. We couldn't meet during the lunch hour in the afternoon, because at that time I used to attend my prayers.

Knowing that I was fasting, she also stopped having food which I came to know from a friend of mine. They told me that she came to the lunch hall, but gave her box to her friends and just spent time in the canteen and left for classes.

My respect for her doubled after knowing about her fasting in the holy month.

Today is 17th day of Ramadan, after the afternoon prayers, I went to college and waited for Bhoomi. Once she came out of the classes, I just waved my hand and asked her to wait for me. She nodded her head as a sign of acceptance and waved her hand to her security to wait for her to return. I reached her meanwhile.

"What's happened Sameer? Why did you suddenly come over?" she asked.

"Nothing happened, I just came to meet you because it's been 17 days since we met, so I thought of meeting you today," I replied.

"Why? For what Sameer? Why would you want to meet me? Huh," she got angry. Seeing her reaction, I was worried.

"I've just come to meet you in a friendly way, Bhoomi, there's no other intention than that," I whispered.

"What do you mean by the other intention? Am I not a good looking girl? Am I not worthy to be loved or liked?" she asked.

"Ayyo! You have got me absolutely wrong. It doesn't mean that. Yes, you're beautiful and a lot of people are going to die for you but because of your father, nobody has the courage to share their feelings with you," I said.

"Are you one of them too?" she immediately asked.

Suddenly after listening to it I fumbled and said no.

If there was a chance, I would have proposed her but I was afraid of her father and kept quiet. She was also very furious and asked questions one after the other.

"No, what does that mean? If you don't feel anything special about me at all, why did you ask me to stop? If someone sees me here with you what are they going to feel about me?" she questioned.

"Nobody's going to feel bad about you, everyone here knows that you're a great woman with a great character, don't worry," I said.

"And why I asked you to stop is because I got to know you were fasting for Ramadan, so I wanted to thank you for respecting our tradition. But don't do it because it's not that easy to go on for 30 days," I said, "Stop doing it."

"Don't tell me what to do and what not to," she said, "mind your job."

"What went wrong? Did I make any mistake, Bhoomi? Why are you being so serious? I'm just asking you to stop for the sake of your good, but why are you doing this?" I asked.

"Do I need to explain all this to you? Who are you to me?" she asked.

Shock after shock, I never expected it and I couldn't answer any of her questions. I couldn't understand why she was so serious and what was the reason behind it.

"Alright Bhoomi, for your health's sake I said it all, rest is your wish. And I'm sorry," I said, "if I hurt you for anything."

She said alright very seriously and left.

I was more confused and I couldn't really understand what mistake I made. I just scratched my head and looked at her, she just turned to me, smiled and got into the car. I got even more confused with that smile.

I left for home with quite a lot of confusion. The afternoon of the next day, before lunch hour, Bhoomi came to my classroom and asked me to meet her after prayer.

This time I was really pissed off and I didn't know how to react and I said I didn't want to meet her.

"Hello, do you realise who you are saying 'NO' to? If my dad gets to know the same thing, do you know what your situation would be?" she said.

She uses her father every time to panic me, and I decided to stick to my statement and say no to whatever happens.

"If you feel like, I've made a mistake and I am not supposed to have my own approach, you can complain to your father. You've got all the freedom and choice, please go ahead, but now I'm not going to meet you after prayer," I said.

"You are serious? Shall I go ahead?" she asked.

"Yeah, please go ahead and don't irritate me anymore. Please, I'm not supposed to get furious with anyone in this holy month," I said.

"Hmm......," she said and just smiled at me.

I couldn't understand why she smiled at me in that strange situation.

"Hey.. Why do you just smile? Gone mad?" I asked.

"Hey Sameer, stop yaar! Since yesterday I was just making fun of you and you are getting worse. I didn't know you were so dumb that you couldn't understand a girl's intention. I wasn't serious at all with you, I was just pretending to be serious and you couldn't figure it. This is so much fun," she grinned, "*haha.*"

With Bhoomi's jovial behaviour, I couldn't say a word but felt sorry for myself acting like a fool.

"Hey, please forgive me, I was joking. Don't take it to heart, Sameer, please," she requested with a cute face.

Who was going to say no to a cute girl who asked them to forgive them. Besides, I was not angry with her.

"It's okay, Bhoomi. I've just become a fool," I said and laughed.

"Hey, I respected your advice as you told me yesterday and I am not going to fast from today. Now be happy," she said. "But I have a request, please get me the kheer and biryani every evening, once you break your fast," she said.

"All right, sure," I said with a smile.

From then on, everyday my mother prepared everything at home a little extra to send to Bhoomi and her dad.

I just spent the whole month praying and fasting. I went to college less frequently, but I didn't miss going to Bhoomi's home. Days went by and Eid arrived. The day before Eid, Bhoomi's dad gave my dad new clothes and a bonus.

Bhoomi Missing

Bhoomi started to come to college in a rickshaw. I wanted to ask her about her experience, but she didn't meet me. I couldn't find her in the college as well.

I inquired about her in her class and her friends told me that she had left after the class. But they had no idea what happened and where was she had gone.

Whom could I ask? Where to find her? I didn't understand, I only had one choice and that was to go to her home and check. So I went to her house.

When I reached her house, her father, my dad and other people were sitting in front of the house and talking something. My father came to me after seeing me there and asked what I was doing there.

I said that I needed some money to buy books.

"Why did you come this long, just for this? You should have asked your mom," he replied.

I was just listening but not concentrating on what he was telling me. I was looking for Bhoomi to get a glimpse of her at least once, but I couldn't see her. And when her father was there, I couldn't go inside.

My dad gave me money and asked me to leave. I went back, dissatisfied. At her home, I couldn't find her and I didn't know where she was. I didn't want to go back to college in that mood so I went straight home.

"Kya Beta? tu itna jaldi wapis aagaya college sey?"

(Son, why did you come back from college early?) Ma asked. *"tumhara tabhyath toh theek hain?"* (Is all well with your health?) she touched my forehead and checked my temperature.

"Nothing Ma, Bhoomi left the college early today and she wasn't at home either," I said.

"So what to worry? She must have gone to her friends," she said.

"No, Ma. No. She does not go to anybody's house. Because of her father, no one dares to call her to their homes. And she has never done so before," I told.

"Something is fishy, she just started to come to college in a private rickshaw for a couple of days and now this is what has happened. I 'm worried about her now," I said.

"Look, now stop thinking. She's Trinath Sharma 's daughter and nobody dares to hurt her. Have some food now and be cool. Anyhow we will get to know about this by evening once your dad gets home," Ma said.

I told my mother okay and went in and freshened up. But Bhoomi 's thoughts continued to haunt me from within. I couldn't help myself at home so I went back to college and asked her classmates about her return again. But they didn't have a positive answer that I was expecting. I went and called Girish.

"Dude, why are you not in class today?" he asked.

"Not in a mood to listen to today's class," I replied.

"Hmmmm. What happened, man? Isn't your girl here today?" he asked.

Well, I just stared at him.

"No, man. She came but left early in the first hour. And nobody knows where she has gone," I said.

"Hmmm, it's interesting. I think she bunked the class and went along with her boyfriend," said Girish.

Now this guy gave me a heart attack. If it was true, then what can I do? It will be more than disappointing. I can't question her, either.

I sat down on the floor, a bit frustrated.

"Hey, man, I was just kidding, don't worry. Tomorrow, when she comes back to college, we are going to get to know where she went," he said.

Yeah, right, but, huh. Sigh.

"I don't know what to say, let's go and have a chai at the canteen," I said.

We went to the canteen, had a cup of tea and waited for the college to get over and go back home. Around 6:30 PM. dad came home and he was in his usual self. I hinted my mom to ask him about Bhoomi, she nodded and told me to be calm. I was curious to know what was happening.

My mother came and asked me, "Why are you so worried, Sameer? If something happened there, do you think your dad 's going to be so cool? So don't worry, she must have returned home. Go and visit your girlfriend tomorrow," she said.

The Unlucky Me

I saw Bhoomi sitting on the steps before I got to college. I just parked the scooter and went to her and asked her about her missing yesterday.

She took me to the hill where she liked to spend time about which she had told me a couple of times. She showed me a tree in which both our names were engraved, and she proposed her love to me.

I did a somersault in my mind with joy, but acted like I wouldn't accept her proposal nor understand why she was doing it.

I know that love is a pure feeling that can't be created or forced, but I couldn't accept her love, because both our status, our caste and our religions didn't match and society would never accept it. Most importantly, her father wouldn't let us marry at all.

I knew my behavior was going to break her heart and cause her pain and frustration, but I was helpless.

She was hurt and cried a lot after my rejection. I wanted to comfort her, but I couldn't. She just needed me to accept her love and make her happy, which I couldn't do.

I said inside, 'how can I convey to you Bhoomi how much I love you? These social constraints are not allowing me to express it. How to describe how happy I am from within after realizing that you also love me, and how difficult it is to reject you. I know you're taking all the pain, but I'm taking twice as much as yours', I just consoled myself and begged her to go back home.

She became very angry and told me she didn't need any support from me. I was trying to make her agree and come home by yelling and scolding although I didn't want to, but I was too helpless. After a couple of failures, I left from there.

After I left, she cried badly. It was my mistake and because of me she's not happy. But God, why did you hurt her because of me? I was happy to love her but after realizing that she too started loving me, I really started to hate myself.

I hid in the vicinity and watched her from there. I waited for her to board the rickshaw. After she left, I came home with a heavy heart. Upon looking at my mother, I burst out. I started to cry.

"Sameer, what the hell happened *beta*? why are you crying?" she questioned me in shock, wiping out my tears.

"Maa! Bhoomi started to love me and she proposed me today," and I cried out louder.

"*Pagal*, this is the time to celebrate, but why are you crying?" she said.

"Maa, you don't understand the reality. If she loves me also, I can't express my feelings and my dad is a servant to her dad, where our status, our caste and our religion will not allow us to marry. Why Maa? why is our marriage system designed in this way? The feeling of love never sees the status, caste or religion. It's a pure feeling that blossoms without any reference checks. Now, because of these rules, we've been separated," I started to cry.

"I know *beta*, it's a pure feeling that you've had for her since childhood, but now all these rules are coming between you two. But I would suggest that you accept her love, and later we can talk to her dad. Who knows, he may accept your love," she said.

"No, Maa, we've been watching him since childhood, he's going to die for his honor and integrity. If he gets to know his daughter loves a Muslim man, then he will kill us both and kill himself but will never accept our relationship," I said.

"So what to do now? He respects his caste and religion more than his own daughter, what are your plans? How many days are you going to cry and sit at home like this?" she asked.

"I'm all right, maa. I know that my love is not going to have a happy ending, but my concern is all about Bhoomi, how to console her and make her understand. I 'm concerned of her. What is she going to do with this disappointment?" I wiped my tears.

"I know her, she's a very strong and brave girl. She can handle it, you don't worry about it," she said.

After the discussion, I never saw Bhoomi in college. Her friends didn't know why she was not coming to college. I was the person responsible behind it. I made her sad and I was roaming peacefully in the campus.

The Acceptance

There was an announcement from the principal saying that everyone must immediately go to Trinath Sharma 's house. No reason was given. My pulse doubled in doubt as to whether she committed suicide. Why did he call everybody there all of a sudden?

We all rushed there, everybody was tensed to see the wrath of Trinath Sharma but I was double worried to know what actually happened. He asked the principal about the absence of his daughter from college and our principal explained that to him. They even called the rickshaw puller to enquire. But my tension didn't end. Bhoomi was not visible anywhere. Was she there or not? Nobody knew.

Bhoomi's father asked my father to send me in to talk to her. So, I asked her father to allow everyone to leave and I went to talk to her personally to get the answer. Because I only knew what had exactly happened.

Firstly, I was relieved because she was at home and I was going to meet her in a couple of minutes. I didn't have any idea how to handle it, but nobody else could help us, so I had to deal it that day.

I walked into her room and saw her weeping in a corner, her eyes swollen. She had became thin and tired. She kept her hair loose without combing them and looked lost.

I asked her why she had behaved that way and stopped eating and coming to college. I asked her to start having food and come to college to talk about rest. She refused and was extremely angry with me. She asked me to accept her love. She said then she would do whatever I said.

Again, I tried to explain everything that she wasn't ready to listen to as she had made up her mind. She asked me to sit near her and when I sat there, she suddenly kissed my lips.

Although I had feelings for her, for a couple of days I rejected the thought of being in a relationship with her. But then the situation went out of control and she had stopped eating. If she continued the same way, she would die. It was better to die for love than starving, so by accepting her love, I decided to save her. I grabbed and pulled her face toward me, kissed her and accepted her love.

She came into her normal self with my acceptance and her father was grateful for that.

My life totally changed after she came into my life. She took so many decisions to make my life better and I was happy for that.

I used to go directly to her father's home without any fear, as he had given me permission to visit her after I had helped her come back.

I gradually became a significant person to their family and I used to be a part of every celebrations. They used to always invite us. Bhoomi was on cloud nine because her father hadn't put any constraints on us and we were really free to move around without any problems. I was happy because Bhoomi was happy. My mother was happy because we both were happy.

Bhoomi 's father never questioned us, we thought he has to know about our relationship and that he must be waiting for it to be revealed by us. So we decided to reveal it once my final exams were over, so we kept our relationship going quietly.

We were enjoying our love journey happily and all of a sudden Bhoomi asked me to take part in the college election as she wanted to see me as president of the college before I left the college. I wasn't ready to participate but she forced me to do it.

I finally accepted and challenged Jagadeesh whom I had followed. He was mad at my behavior.

With a huge majority I won the election and took an oath at a huge gathering. I was happily accepted by the entire college as President. I and Bhoomi spent some time together after the oath ceremony and that was the last time I saw her and spoke to her.

I went back home as usual after I dropped her home. My father came home really serious at about 10 PM. and asked ma to pack all the luggage.

"What happened Ji? Where are we going and why?" ma asked.

"What's more to happen, all because of your stupid son. Sharma sacked me out of work and warned us to leave town by morning," dad yelled.

"What did I do dad? Why do we have to get out of town?" I asked.

"You Bastard, are you still acting like nothing has happened? Haven't you messed up with Bhoomi?" dad slapped me.

"Messed up? What the hell are you talking about, dad? And why did you just hit me?" I raised my voice at my father.

"Why are you both arguing? What is actually going on, can anyone explain it to me?" my ma cried out.

"What more can I explain? This fool is in love with Sharma's Daughter and he came to know about it through Jagadeesh today. He slapped her and locked her at home. He gave us an ultimatum to leave the city. Do you need more details about this? If you want to die in his lap, you can live here," he told me and asked my mom to pack up as soon as possible.

After knowing the truth, my mom started crying.

We had no choice but to leave the town. That idiot, Jagadeesh, didn't let us have any choice to negotiate at least. He ruined it. We packed and left the city at night.

That night had been a nightmare for me to handle the truth that Sharma had slapped and locked Bhoomi. I couldn't digest it, but I was powerless and unable to deal with it.

We moved to my mamu's house after leaving the city. I had gone through depression. I came to college a few times wearing a mask and met Girish to find out about Bhoomi, but there was no information about her.

After I left college, Jagadeesh became the president again and made strict rules for the students and began to torture them as they supported me.

Months passed, but there was no information that I could get about Bhoomi. My father told me that Sharma had closed all his business and that Jagadeesh and his father had begun to do all the things and had become pretty powerful.

Girish only knows where I was living and what I was doing and has been trying to find out the details about Bhoomi. During this idle period, my father and I became very close and he understood my situation and the reason for our love and Jagadeesh's cheating.

"Sameer, now Trinath Sharma has shut all his business not because of his sorrow about his daughter but because he doesn't have my support with him. Those days people were afraid of him because we were with him, not just because of who he was. We sacrifice our lives for our leaders, and they enjoy the name and fame. What we get at the end of the day is disrespect and expatriation from society. It is high time we teach them a lesson that if any common man is turned down by the leader, his empire will crumble."

"Hearing about your story, I don't think it is wrong. You just get the details about your girl. I'm going to help you to get her out of her home," dad said.

I just burst out in tears hugging him after listening to my dad's support. Those many days, I had held back my tears without sharing it with anyone. Because elders say men shouldn't cry but they also have feelings and they have tears too.

The Evacuation Plan

I showed the letter to dad and he told me that we were going to go to Sharma 's house the next day and get Bhoomi. Ok, I embraced it. My father told Jagadeesh's father to support him in the matter because he was close to him. Few of my dad's friends also joined us to attack Sharma's house to get Bhoomi.

We all started going to Sharma's house. If we were going together, someone might tell him that a lot of people were coming to attack and he might escape from there, so my dad had the idea to split up in small batches and meet at a place before we got there.

As planned, we split up into small batches and started. My father and Jagadeesh's team had gone before and I and some of my dad's friends went together.

"Sameer, what you've done isn't correct," one of my dad's friends said.

"What happened uncle? What the hell did I do?" I asked.

"Loving the daughter of Sharma. And now you're involving your dad in this matter," he said.

"Oh, Calm down, uncle. My dad's helping me after recognizing our love, before he was against it," I said.

"Your father was a very nice person who fought against crime. You know, we used to work with Sharma too, but for a few reasons he removed us and asked your father to kill us, but he never did it. Instead he told us to stay away from the city and gave us a second life. Today, in that respect, we have come to support your father, but not you," he said.

After knowing my father's greatness, I felt very lucky to be his son. I thanked them for coming, and told them that I was not going to give him any more stress after that.

"He has set some rules of life for himself, which he never crossed for anyone and he follows them until today. But for the first time, he sacrificed all his good practices for you alone," he said.

After I knew his greatness, I felt pitied myself because only for me he had abandoned his philosophy, which he had followed throughout his life.

I decided to give my parents a peaceful life that they had just sacrificed for my freedom after my marriage.

At least from now on, they deserved to be happy and enjoy the rest of their lives.

"We 're happy about what you've done, and what your dad is doing for you. At least now Sharma is going to get his vengeance for his sins. He enjoyed the power till today all because of us and when we made any small mistake, he ordered to kill us and killed a few amongst us. Now, who's going to save his pride, we want to see too," he said.

We were talking while we advanced to the place where we had all planned to meet. I could see a guy who had fallen on the field while the rest of us were all standing and looking at him.

As I approached them, I could see clearly that the person who fell on the field was my dad. I just jumped out of the scooter and ran to my dad.

"Daddy, what happened to you? Who did this to you? Dad, look at me?" I cried loudly while holding my dad.

"Jagadeesh, who did it to my dad? Tell me, why was he just attacked? Why didn't you take him to the doctor?" I asked.

Everyone was quiet, my dad's friends became silent and furious and they made up their minds to kill Sharma. He only must have planned to do all these. No one else was responding from the side of Jagadeesh. I wiped my tears and questioned Jagadish.

"What dude? Why are you so quiet? What did you people do until my father was stabbed by someone? Answer me."

Jagadeesh started laughing, "Poor, Sameer! Who dares to come here to stab your dad after seeing us? I only stabbed him. You motherfucker! You destroyed my reputation in college and now you want to marry Bhoomi too? How can we let you marry a girl of our religion? All this strategy is to destroy you both and we've done it very well. Your power is gone now. It is easy to clear you," he said.

They had cheated us and killed my father and knowing that boiled my blood. Whatever he did wearing the fake mask of friendship, I wasn't ready to forgive it.

"Uncle, my father was killed by these bastards and nobody should abandon the ground today. Chop their heads to pieces. I want to see their end now," I demanded.

"I didn't react when my love was destroyed by this bastard, but now he has killed my father and I am not going to leave him alone," I told my father's friends.

"We were also waiting to see your end. Come on! There should be only one king and that should be me," said Jagadeesh's father.

I just placed my father's head gently on the ground and ran toward Jagadeesh to kill him but he escaped and hit me on my back as he was a strong guy. I violently dropped down to the ground. He started hitting my head by the time I recovered, without giving me time. My skin was ruptured and I started bleeding. My eyes were swollen and instead of tears, I started shedding blood.

I endured all the pain and started shouting, "Hit me hard and kill me now! If you're going to give me some time to settle, then you're going to be sorry, I'm going to kill you in one blow."

"You! You are gonna kill me, huh? Chalo Chalo.. I'm giving you time to settle down. First, you stand up and show me, later you can kill me," he challenged me and began to laugh.

I was watching my father's friends clearing most of his team. I could see the scattered bodies of Jagadeesh 's men all over. I needed to regain all my energy now and kill both of those bastards.

I remembered all my past, the sacrifice my father had made, Bhoomi's love and Jagadeesh's deceit. After I remembered all those, my eyes teared, I cried out for my incompetence. But if I loose my confidence and surrendered, I, Bhoomi and her father will also be killed. I had to fight until my last breath. I decided.

I managed to get up and sit on the ground with all my power. After I sat on the ground the very next moment Jagadeesh kicked me on my head. I just fell down to the ground. Blood dripped from my hair and fell drop by drop onto the ground.

Jagadeesh's father came to me and holding my shirt collar, pulled me up. Raising my two hands and holding them, he asked Jagadeesh to stab me.

I could see the smile on Jagadeesh 's face with my eyes slightly opened. In his eyes, reflected his winning moment. But I was too sad of my loss. All I gained from love and sacrifice was nothing. I had lost my family, and my future. Whatever I did was wrong, but it was too late to realize that then. I could see my death quite clearly. It ran to me in the form of Jagadeesh, I embraced it as a loser and closed my eyes and gave up.

Then I heard Jagadeesh's painful cry and him begging for forgiveness in pain. I didn't understand what had happened. I opened my eyes with curiosity. I could see a clear picture of my father standing there and finishing off Jagadeesh. Within a moment's blink of an eye, he moved towards us and cleared Jagadeesh's father.

My father hugged me and wiped all of the blood from my face. In a very low voice, I said vaguely, "Sorry dad". He Smiled.

"Son, whatever we began, it has to end with our generation, you shouldn't be a part of that. They were trying to kill me and I killed them. It's over now. I don't like you to be a part of all this unethical business. My death is unpredictable and unstoppable. I know I'm going to die. You go home, take care of your mother and get married to your love and be happy," he placed his hand on my head, blessed me and died.

I cried a lot. He died a heroic death after battling a force that was cruel. I carried him on my shoulder and brought him home. My mother could not digest the truth of his death. We had his last rights finished.

To heal fully from all my wounds, I took almost 6 months. So many times, with the aid of Girish, I tried to go see Bhoomi, but my mother did not allow me to step out of my home. I finally went to see Bhoomi after 6 months, but by that time it was too late and everything had changed there forever.

A few others had occupied the house. They told me that Trinath Sharma had died and Bhoomi had sold the property and left after that. They didn't know where she was and they didn't have any clue about it.

I went home disappointed. I searched every possible place for her, but I got disappointed every time. I completed my studies and worked as a lecturer in a government job. I started my career and became a good lecturer who was a favorite to many students in a very short time.

My mom asked me so many times to get married but I refused. After a while she stopped asking me.

In a deputation, I got a transfer from Andhra University to Osmania University. So my mother and I shifted to Hyderabad. Then my mother passed away after 10 years and I became lonely. I decided to sell all my property and move to an old age home as I became old.

This is the story behind that letter to which I couldn't respond. He said wiping tears from his eyes.

Female Block

"Sir, the tear in your eyes melted me and we can understand the pain that you hold inside you. Do you still love her? If you find out about her current address, what will you do?" I asked.

"Yes, I am going to love her until my last breath. But I regret not answering her letter. If I get to know her address, I ' m going to go and convey her my apology and come back, then I'm going to die in peace," he answered.

"Why will you come back sir? Won't you stay with her?" I asked.

"Boy..! What's your name?" he asked.

"George," I said.

"Ha..! George, how do you think I will live with her? It's been thirty eight years since we've been apart, and she must be married to someone and would be leading a happy life. Now I can love her secretly, but I don't think I'll stay with her," he said.

I bit my tongue, because he didn't know the other side of the story. Oh yeah, I said.

"Sir, after listening to your love story, like you, I'm sure she also might be waiting for you without getting married," I said.

"There should be a limit for dumbness, my boy, it will be very difficult as a girl to live alone, without any protection. And I didn't expect this to ruin her life for me."

"Alright sir, I need to tell you the truth now. We met Ms. Bhoomi before we came to you and got to know the other side of your story and the rest we understood from you," I said.

While listening to it, he suddenly turned to me and asked, "What you were saying? Have you met Bhoomi? Where is she? When? What is she doing?" with excitement, he began to ask questions.

"Relax, sir," I offered him some water and asked him to sit down. He quickly gulped the water, and asked about Bhoomi. Then I explained the whole story of what happened after I had found the letter. He realized that she was staying in the same old-age home in the female block.

"Rudrayya…. Rudrayya!" he shouted loudly. The watchman came running very tensed to his room.

"What's wrong sir? Why did you just call me?"

"Do we have a lady called Bhoomi in the female block?" he asked him.

"Yes , sir, Bhoomi Ma'am, she is only running this home," watchman said.

"Just take me to her right now," he said.

"Maam isn't here, sir, she went on her usual evening walk 15 minutes ago. She'll be back in an hour," the watchman replied.

Sameer waited all his life for her without any anxiety, but this one hour wait was the most difficult part of his life and I could feel that. We also waited there to see the happy ending of their story.

On Sameer sir's face, I could see both happiness and tension at the same time. He moved from one corner to the other restlessly to cover up his emotions.

After nearly 38 years, he was preparing himself to meet the love of his life. He looked like a hero. Bhoomi would certainly be happy to see him then.

"Rudrayya... " called Sameer.

"Sir, tell me," he said.

"Go and get a bouquet of red roses," he said offering him 500 rupees.

He picked up the money and left. Three of us stood there watching a young lover boy in a 60 years old Sameer. We were overwhelmed to see that beautiful scene.

We were happy to be a part of a sad love story to end in this happy note. We understood that day that every of our action has a solid reason behind it. There is a supreme power than the one in our imagination which runs the universe which is super power.

Destiny is all set for us, it's already decided, but we're fighting to win in all forms. We don't know that our struggle is also a part of the act that super-power directs us from the space where our imagination can't reach. In our lives, every individual plays his or her role and leaves, we fight each other, we blame each other for the things that happen in the journey of our lives. Our laughter, our sorrow, our humor is all part of the act of life.

Who are we? Why did I find that letter? Out of so many people who had returned the purse previously, why was only I who was fascinated to know the story behind it? Why did we drive so long to get to know the story? Is he leading us from there to help them finally meet and finish their happy story? I didn't know what it was and who was behind it, but, today, their long wait was coming to an end and the rest of their lives were going to be happy forever.

Whenever you're waiting for something beautiful to happen, time doesn't move fast. It gives a new heart attack every second. We, four of us, were waiting for the time to move quickly and Bhoomi to enter the gate. Our eight eyes were fixed on the Old Age home gate waiting curiously to see her there.

Time was approaching and Rudrayya had reached back with red roses. Our heart beats had touched the sky. We didn't know how Sameer was feeling in that situation.

"Sir, we want a little break, we haven't been able to control our stress, please may we?" we asked for permission and went out to smoke.

We went to a nearby pan shop and lit a cigarette.

"What is this man, Joseph? I have never faced this curiosity and tension before. How could a couple feel to meet after 38 years?" I said.

"Hmmm… Rey, I'm going to die for sure, give me a quick puff of cigarette, you idiot! Stop asking questions," Joseph yelled.

Passing my cigarette over to him, I said, "I've never experienced it before, man. It's a whole new thing and the most exciting," I said.

While we were discussing this in tension, I could hear the ambulance siren passing ahead of us. While inhaling the cigarette smoke, I saw a gathering almost 300 meters from us.

After looking at it, I was silent. Since I was already going through a lot of anxiety, I didn't want to divert into another tension then. But somewhere in my subconscious mind it squeezed me from within and pushed me to the incident to check it out.

I inhaled the last cigarette puff and raced to the place where the incident had taken place. Joseph and Ananya were shocked with the act. They didn't know why I was running and followed me.

Just in minutes we reached there, an elderly lady has fallen down there and the ambulance staff were giving her first aid. A lot of people had gathered and we couldn't see her very clearly. We inquired about the incident and realized that she had collapsed due to low blood pressure. We realized that she wasn't in a serious condition and we started back to the Old Age Home.

Nevertheless, I was not satisfied and my inner soul asked me to see the lady first, who had collapsed before I left. I caught the hand of Ananya and asked them to stop. Both were then confused and were asking me what happened?

I doubted that the lady was Bhoomi. We just needed to see her before they took her to the ambulance. God had different plans for her, he never let those beautiful couples meet. This time, too, he had to play a game with their poor lives, we had to break all his plans.

"Joseph, please go and check, I'm a thousand percent sure, she's only Bhoomi. Go and check," I insisted.

Unintentionally, my eyes began to tear as I could see a clear end to the story where Bhoomi would not know about Sameer. She will not know that the love of her life was waiting at the gate with red roses to propose to her again and to give an answer to her letter. Why was I crying? I didn't have anything to do with either of these two, why was I getting emotional? Yes, this is the magic of love, everyone will feel that pain once you've gone through it. I was angry at God for the first time. Why was he doing this? Was he doing this because he has more powers than us? They were already given a lot of pain that they had already taken, and now had entered their last stage of life. They sacrificed their whole life for love, now that God is still punishing them, I felt sorry for them.

In the meantime, Joseph came and confirmed that my guess was correct and that Bhoomi was the lady. I just wiped my tears and asked Ananya to accompany Bhoomi in the ambulance and share the hospital details with us so that we could get Sameer there.

Once the ambulance started, we went back to Sameer. But I had so many thoughts and questions in my mind as I walked back. How to tell Sameer the truth? Will he be able to take it at this age? He was the happiest person before we got out of here, but if we tell him, will he collapse? What to do, then?

Do we have any other choice left? No, we've got to take him to the Hospital before it's too late.

We were able to convey the situation we saw on the road with full courage and strength. I thought that since he had seen all the struggles and failures throughout his life, he would be weak to receive this. But he proved us wrong, and he was strong and said, "Let's go to the hospital."

Epilogue

Everyone was rushing around in the hospital, but four of us were standing outside the ICU waiting for the doctor to come out and announce the status.

Sameer held in his hand the rose flowers, leaning on the wall and looking at the roof. I knew how he was feeling then. Within his heart thousands of volcanoes must have erupted. He mustn't have thought he would find his love in that situation. He was happy till today as he thought somewhere she was happy in his imagination. But it was very difficult to realize that she was at the ICU, fighting for her life.

He understood the true meaning of love and with the roses he wanted to express his love for her that day. Once he learned that she had been admitted to the hospital, he didn't leave the roses there but still held onto them. He knew the strength of his love for her. He was confident that he would meet his love and express his feelings and respond to her letter.

I felt pity for our generation looking at him. If we don't see our girlfriend or boyfriend for a month, we'll find a replacement for them. But he was very dedicated and genuine to his love even at this age. He had really got ready as if he was still young to meet her. There is no specific age for love.

Joseph brought Sameer some water and a coffee. Ananya continuously engaged him in conversation so as not to lose hope. We were trying all ways to keep him engaged until the doctor stepped out.

Then, the doctor came and explained that she had a brain hemorrhage that led to her collapse and unconsciousness. "We did an MRI, it was just a small blood clot in the brain that could be cured with medicine. We'll put her here for 24 hours in the ICU and monitor any other complications that may arise. No need to worry now as she is responding to the medicine, you can go and check her out," he said.

After listening to the doctor we are more nervous than Sameer. But Sameer asked us, "Son, how many days we 're going to live? So don't think about what's killing us from the inside, but be content that with more and more love we 're meeting and enjoying the rest of our lives. The remainder of our lives would be the equal as the ones we spent."

I hugged Sameer and said, "Sir, it is now your turn to give your love the answer. She's been waiting for your answer for 38 years. We've been afraid to know she's fallen down. I thought, she would leave the world without your answer, but I'm wrong sir. My guess is a little thing in front of your true love and now you have to make her smile."

We went to the ICU. She was resting with the oxygen mask on. Sameer sat just next to her and placed the roses on the bed next to her. He gently held her hand to adjust his spectacles.

I don't know the magic, but the next moment he touched her, she opened her eyes and saw him.

She only removed the oxygen supply with her left hand and called Sameer in a painful tone. Her eyes were crying with joy. The wait of 38 years, the suffering that she must have gone through, the blame that she must have suffered from society, all that we could recognize in her voice. She missed him a lot and waited for him her entire life.

Sameer wiped her eyes and kissed her forehead, and said, "Now why are you crying? You've got to be happy, your Sameer is here for you. You know, I don't like to see you cry. No matter what pain we have gone through, it's enough for our life. The rest of it must be happy."

She nodded happily in acceptance of it.

"I know I've given you more pain your entire life without responding to your letter. You were still waiting for me to come," Sameer explained what had actually happened after the letter of Bhoomi.

"Sameer, why do you explain all this to me? I know my Sameer, who never makes a mistake. And there must be a strong reason for your failure to respond to my letter. And I'm not waiting to hear all the explanations," Bhoomi replied.

"I know, but it's my responsibility to explain what happened. Okay, I'm not going to say that, but I need to reply to the letter you wrote otherwise it will remain unanswered."

"Yes , sir, even we 're waiting for your response to that," I said.

After listening to me, Bhoomi smiled.

Sameer gently placed Bhoomi's hand on the bed, rose from the stool and put his hand in the pocket. He took out a ring and stood on his knee and asked, "Will you marry me?"

After he asked her to marry, Bhoomi began to cry. She was wiping her tears and said Okay to his proposal.

He put the ring on her finger and kissed her. We clapped in excitement and joy. All the staffs and patients of the ICU were shocked and warned us to leave.

Sameer said, "I love you, Bhoomi." And Bhoomi said, "I love you too."

With a smile on all our faces, we walked out of the ICU.

9 7 9 8 6 6 6 0 2 2 1 4 6